VOLUME FOUR

AIRSHIP 27 PRODUCTIONS

Domino Lady-Volume Four

"Diamonds are the Lady's Best Friend" ©2022 Gene Moyers
"Three Dead Men" ©2022 Kelly Nolan
"Blue Sapphires and Platinum Blondes" ©2022 Kevin Findley
"Domino Lady Deceived" ©2022 Samantha Lienhard

Published by Airship 27 Productions
www.airship27.com
www.airship27hangar.com

Cover illustration ©2022 Ted Hammond
Interior illustrations ©2022 James Lyle

Editor: Ron Fortier
Associate Editor: Gordon Dymowski
Marketing and Promotions Manager: Michael Vance
Production Designer: Rob Davis.

ISBN: 978-1-953589-23-1

Printed in the United States of America

10 9 8 7 6 5 4 3 2 1

Domino Lady

Volume Four
Table of Contents

Diamonds Are the Lady's Best Friend

Gene Moyers

Ellen leaned closer to the hard metal surface. Sweat beaded her forehead and she bit her lip in concentration as she slowly turned the large Bakelite knob. It was warm and stuffy in the nearly darkened room. Silence surrounded her, the only sound her labored breathing as she focused on the dial. The serrations on the knob's surface were slippery and she stopped to rub her fingertips on a shapely, cotton draped thigh before returning them to the knob.

A voice from behind her broke the silence startling her, "Now Darlin' why would ye' be leaning closer to the safe door. Ye're nae gonna be hearing the tumblers no matter how close ye get. Ye' have to feel them! Close ye're eyes and use ye're fingers. Their pretty enough, use 'em for something useful."

Ellen stood up from her crouch, turned and glared at the short, gray haired, slightly built man sitting behind her on a stool. He was leaning forward and squinting hard at her. Ellen blew upward, flipping a stray lock of long blonde hair that had fallen over her forehead out of the way and glared at the little man, "Easy for you to say, Fitz. This isn't easy, as you well know." She paused for a moment before demanding, "And why is it so blasted hot in here?"

Sean Fitzsimmons, retired safe cracker and graduate of Auburn and Joliet chuckled quietly, "And do ye' think all the safes ye'll be opening will be in the parlor with a cool breeze blowing through the open window? Ye'll nae be workin' in pleasant conditions. It'll likely be just as hot and dark as here, worse more like. Now get back to it, lass. And use ye're fingers; feel the tumblers. Close ye're eyes, it'll help."

She gave the little man a hard look, then turned back to the safe set in a false wall, muttering under her breath. Leaning close to the dial, Ellen closed her eyes and reached for the dial. Instead of straining her ears, she concentrated on her fingers, attempting to feel the slightest imperfection as she slowly turned the dial. Moments later, she felt the slightest catch as she turned the dial to the left. Was that something? She froze, then deciding it was significant she turned the dial back to the right. When

5

she again felt a hesitation in the movement of the dial, she once more reversed direction in her turning. Finally, she stopped. She had definitely felt something metallic move under her fingers that time.

Standing up, she stretched her back and then grasped the metal safe handle. With a jerk she turned it sharply ninety degrees upward and pulled the small safe door open. Turning to her teacher with a triumphant grin she exclaimed, "Got it!"

The gray-haired ex-thief held a stop watch up to his face and squinted at the face for a long moment. Hopping off the stool, he shook his head and remarked, "Aye, and high time. Me aged Mum could have done better and she's eighty years old and crippled, bless her soul."

Wiping her face with a handkerchief from her purse, Ellen glared at the old man, "I was faster than last week, you old coot!"

Fitz's aged face crinkled in laughter as said, "Tis' true, lass. Ye're improving every week. Although I still canna understand why ye' wanna crack safes. Anyone can see that ye're no thief."

Ellen gathered up her purse and coat saying, "Now, you know our agreement: no questions and no answers." She stepped forward and took the old man's hand, pressing a ten-dollar bill into it, "Same time next week?"

"Of course, lass. I'll be here. Where would an old crook like meself go?"

He followed Ellen through the back room and down a hall to an outside door. As she opened it and stepped through, she turned back and asked, "Do you miss it much, Fitz?"

The old man thought a moment before sighing, "Aye, there were moments; the excitement and the money—but I spent a lot of time behind walls and bars. No—I would'na go back for all the whiskey in Ireland."

Ellen nodded though the old man couldn't see it, "See you next week." She stepped out into the alley, turned right and walked toward the street.

"God be with ye, lass."

Reaching the sidewalk, Ellen turned and walked toward her car. Inside, she pressed the starter and pulled out onto the quiet side street in San Pedro. As she guided the roadster toward Hollywood, she thought back on her lessons with Sean. She had looked long and hard to find the right teacher. Sean fit the bill perfectly. He once had been one of the best safecrackers around. Now he was old and needed money bad enough to take on a young "lass" as a student. Best of all his sight was so bad he could pass her on the street and he wouldn't recognize her.

The lessons were tedious and it seemed to take forever to make any progress, but after several months Ellen was finally getting halfway good at it. Her lock picking skills were good but too many times her plans had been frustrated by locked combination safes. Deciding to remedy this situation she had hunted up a teacher and Sean's weekly lessons were the result. And with the Havelock situation occupying more of her time she knew in her heart that her new skill would soon be put to use.

Back at her Wilshire Blvd apartment, she parked her roadster and was soon greeting the doorman as she crossed the lobby to check her mail box. Moments later she was in the elevator on her way up to her apartment. Once inside, she dropped her purse and keys on a side table and made for the kitchen. Soon, armed with a glass and an open bottle of champagne she made her way out onto the balcony and plopped down in a comfortable lounge chair. The champagne tasted luscious after an afternoon fighting with combination locks. As she toasted her progress she thought about the current target of her skills, new and old: Jason Havelock.

Havelock had come to the Ellen's attention the winter before. She had been quietly looking into the finances of a questionable state politician at the time. Sure enough, she found he was quietly accepting money from a southern California mobster. Investigation of the mobster had led her to Havelock.

Havelock was a well-known southern California financier. He had managed to make money even during the crash and seem to have the "Golden" touch in all his investments. It had taken weeks of investigation to find he was not only laundering money for several well-known mobsters but investing their money as well.

Ellen had arranged an introduction from a mutual friend and had cultivated Havelock and his wife. When not ferreting out his various legitimate business dealings and their locations, she had been following him and his shady acquaintances in the disguise of the mysterious Domino Lady. Preparing for future action against him, she had begun her safecracking lessons.

Things had really come to a boil several weeks before. She had been following Havelock late one spring evening when he had varied from his usual schedule.

The Domino Lady braked her roadster and pulled to the curb. Fifty yards ahead, Havelock's DeSoto town car braked to a halt in front of a row of darkened businesses. Its headlights were extinguished and a moment later Havelock got out of the back. On the sidewalk he had a brief word with his chauffeur before turning and entering a nearby alley. Sensing that the night was about to get interesting Domino Lady quickly slipped on her black mask and got out of her car easing the car door closed behind her. Gathering her black cloak around her to conceal her long white dress, she glided down the street toward the car.

It was after ten o'clock and the West Hollywood street was quiet; its businesses closed and darkened. Easing silently up the street she soon reached a narrow alley next to a shoe store. Twenty feet ahead the town car sat silently. The driver sitting behind the wheel with his back to her. She could smell the smoke from the cigarette he smoked while awaiting his boss' return. Turning into the alley, she wondered what Havelock was doing here at this time of night.

Reaching the wider rear alley running parallel to the street, she waited while her eyes adjusted to the gloom. The alley was in total darkness. The only illumination came from the strip of starry sky over head. Turning, she saw a dim light coming from behind a curtained window in the back wall of the shoe store. There was a door near the window but she ignored it. Instead, she turned to the building across the narrow alley from the shoe store.

This building had a fire escape ladder running up to the second story roof. She found an empty crate nearby and quietly positioned it under the ladder. Hiking up her dress, she climbed on top of the crate to reach the ladder. It wasn't an easy climb in heels and long dress but moments later she was standing on the flat roof.

The roof of the shoe store was nearly four feet away across the narrow alley she had entered by. Taking off her heels, she grasped one in each hand and took four steps backward. Then she sucked in a breath and ran at the gap. Her left foot caught the top of the eight-inch high parapet pushing her outward. Her right foot landed just over the opposing parapet and she leaned forward to keep her momentum and took three quick steps to slow herself down. The roof had felt solid and she had heard barely a thump from her one hundred sixteen pounds landing lightly on the roof.

She quickly scanned the roof and glided silently toward a dimly illuminated skylight. She peered down through the dusty glass but could not make anything out. She dropped to one knee, set down her shoes and rubbed a large spot clear of dust and dead insects. In the back room of the shoe store two men conversed by the dim light of a hooded desk lamp. One sat behind the desk. Havelock, the other, paced back and forth in front of it.

This was too good to miss. Gripping the edge of the skylight frame she gave up a quick prayer and gently lifted. As she had hoped the sky light moved. It was probably opened by someone using a long-handled tool from the floor below and nobody had bothered to latch it. Slipping one of her high heels into the gap, she silently lowered the frame down. With her ear to the three-inch horizontal crack, the men's words came to her clearly.

"That's not enough. I've got to have at least fifty thousand for it," Havelock declared.

"Sorry. It'd take a lot to move a piece like that. Thirty thousand; take it or leave it," replied the stranger.

Havelock complained, "But it's worth over eighty thousand!"

"I'll go thirty-five, not a penny more."

Havelock sounded frustrated as he answered, "That doesn't do me any good. I need fifty thousand."

The stranger's chair creaked as he leaned back, "So, look at it this way. You only need fifteen thousand now. That should help."

Not for what I need it for," gritted Havelock.

Domino Lady thought she detected a note of fear in Havelock's voice mixed in with the frustration. Why was he frightened? More importantly, what were they were bargaining over?

The stranger continued, "So, do we have a deal."

There was a pause before Havelock replied, "I'll have to think about it."

Domino Lady risked a quick glance over the edge of the skylight. The stranger got up from his seat. He and Havelock disappeared out of sight toward the rear of the building. Taking this opportunity, she lifted the frame slightly and slipped her heel out before lowering it again. Creeping to the edge of the roof she heard a door close below her. A look down showed Havelock traversing the narrow alley to the sidewalk in front of the shoe store. Moments later she heard the engine of the DeSoto start up with a growl and then fade slowly away.

Quickly, she jumped back the way she had come. As she replaced her heels before descending the ladder into the alley, a door slammed and a lock clicked below her. Footsteps quickly faded down the alley. On the ground, Domino Lady navigated the alley to the sidewalk. The street was empty. There was no one to see as she returned to her roadster and drove away.

Her thoughts were active as she drove eastward toward her apartment. Why was Havelock trying to fence a valuable object? Where would he have gotten a stolen object worth that much? Fifty thousand was a lot of money, but Havelock dealt in large sums all the time. Did he have money troubles no one suspected? She also thought, "I must keep that address in mind. I didn't know about that fence."

Although Havelock's late-night rendezvous was interesting it didn't make sense until it was put into context by the newspaper headline Ellen Patrick read the next Sunday morning. She was sitting on the balcony taking the sun and sipping coffee when she opened the paper and read: **Wealthy Financier Robbed.** And underneath the sub-headline; "Bell Air mansion burglarized overnight."

The article was informative. It seemed that late the night before, Havelock and his wife had returned to their Bel Air home to find it had been burglarized. The mansion had been unguarded as the chauffeur who doubled as Havelock's bodyguard was with them at the time. No cash was taken but Mrs. Havelock's prize diamond necklace had been stolen along with other jewelry. Police were investigating and expecting a quick arrest. Ellen snickered over that one. They were always expecting quick arrests. Most interesting of all was the description *The LA Times* gave of the necklace and its value. The newspaper valued the necklace at over eighty thousand dollars.

Ellen took a sip of her coffee and thought, "That's a convenient coincidence. Havelock's negotiating with an illegal fence and days later he's robbed of a valuable necklace." She decided to keep a close eye on this development.

The police did not locate the missing necklace nor did they arrest anyone for the crime. No surprise there. And, within a few weeks there was a small one column story in *The Times* stating that Havelock's insurance had paid off on his claim. The story was quickly forgotten by everyone except Ellen. She asked quietly around some of her less socially accepted acquaintances and learned that no one had heard of the missing necklace, despite much speculation that it would turn up, or at least parts of it, on the black market.

Adding this high-profile crime to what she had heard in the back room of the shoe store, she decided that Havelock had robbed himself for the insurance. Why not? It was perfect. He got the full amount of the insurance plus he didn't have to share anything with a fence and he got to keep the necklace. Not that his wife could wear it. The necklace had to be hidden away. If anyone saw it there would be very embarrassing questions asked.

Now Ellen and her alter ego had a highly visible target. She would find the necklace and pin the fraud on Havelock. She knew his habits and haunts. How hard could it be to find the necklace?

It turned out to be quite hard. Ellen sipped champagne and thought of the research and legwork she had done. She had searched several of his properties. Finding several safes, she had put her hard-earned lessons to work. She had also wangled an invitation to a dinner party at the Havelock's. There she had made friends with his wife Barbara who had been glad to give Ellen a guide tour of her home after a few flattering remarks about the decorating.

There was still much to do. Her safecracking skills were improving and she was certain she would locate the necklace soon. There was also the decision of how best to use the necklace when she finally found it. Yes, lots to do.

Ellen was reaching for the bottle to refill her glass when the phone rang. Filling up her glass she went into the hall to answer it, "Hello."

"Ellen, you have to rescue me from all this madness. Are you free tonight?"

Ellen laughed, "Tony, it's good to hear your voice. As a matter of fact, I am free. Although, I can't imagine you needing any rescuing from your sworn duty of keeping Los Angeles safe from dastardly villains and evil doers. What crimes have you prosecuted today? Maybe a juicy murder? Or perhaps you've uncovered evidence of massive corruption at City Hall?"

Her caller replied with mock fear, "Don't say that? Those people sign my paychecks! As for today, I did file some nasty motions and fought through a stack of depositions. So, I've earned a night out."

They both laughed for a moment before her Ellen's latest conquest asked, "So how about dinner and some dancing afterward?"

Ellen feigned boredom, "Well, I did have plans to rid the city of a cruel mobster but I suppose I could make time if you like."

"Great! Pick you up at seven?"

"Fine with me. Don't be late."

"Okay, see you then." Tony hung up as did Ellen, smiling as she did so. She had met Anthony Hulme a few months back. He was a sharp, handsome young assistant District Attorney for the city. He was witty, talented and a fine dancer. All in all, quite a catch if you were looking for a handsome man who was going places. He had told her early on in their relationship that he was planning on being District Attorney in the future as well as state Attorney General someday. Ellen did not doubt him for a second, he had the ambition to match his abilities. He would go far— especially with the proper help.

Glancing at her watch, Ellen decided she had enough time for a nice long bath but then would have to hustle. She started down the hall, stopped and quickly backtracked to the balcony. Grabbing up the half empty champagne bottle and her glass, she then headed for the bathroom humming "I've got the World on a String" as she did.

Tony reluctantly let his arm drop from around Ellen's waist as the music stopped. The two then clapped politely along with many of the dancers. The band immediately launched into another song. Tony held out his arms but Ellen held up hers in self-defense, "I need a break. You can wear a girl out."

Tony put a hand to the small of her back as he guided her back to their table. Dinner at the new *Brown Derby* restaurant in Beverly Hills had been followed by dancing at a Hollywood night club. Tony motioned the waiter for another round of drinks but Ellen waved a hand, "No more, my head is spinning!" Actually, Ellen was fine but she often found it useful to seem less sober than she really was.

As Tony related a humorous story from work, she studied him. She enjoyed his company but she couldn't let herself get carried away. She had to keep her long game in mind at all times.

Finished with his story, Tony asked, "Do you have plans next weekend? I have a lawyer friend who is willing to loan me his boat. I was thinking we might take it out to Catalina for the weekend.

Ellen gave him a demur look, "Why Tony, you didn't tell me you were a yachtsman."

Tony tried to look modest, "Well, I uh . . ."

"While that sounds lovely, I actually had plans to ask you to be my escort next weekend."

A bit surprised Tony replied, "Oh! What did you have planned?"

"Well, I've been invited to a dinner party by Jason and Barbara Havelock. Do you know them? Anyway, I need a handsome gentleman to escort me.

Know anyone who might be interested?"

"Havelock the big shot investor? I didn't know you knew him."

"Oh sure, I had lunch with his wife Barbara just last week. You should have her show you their home. It's wonderful. That is, if you want to go."

"I wouldn't miss it for the world."

"Good. Now, you can take me home. I'm exhausted."

Waving for the check Tony replied, "Anything, you want Princess."

Three nights later, Tony would have been shocked to see his "Princess." The Domino Lady carefully eased out of a broom closet on the eighth floor of the *Curtis Building* downtown. Slipping silently down the hallway to a corner, she edged an eye around it. A uniformed security guard stood waiting for the elevator. When it arrived, the guard stepped in and departed. "Finally!" she mouthed silently before turning and going back the other way. Earlier, she had secreted herself in the woman's restroom on the same floor and waited for foot traffic to die down after the building was closed. She had used this particular trick before and it was generally effective. Unfortunately, a particularly annoying security guard had frustrated her plan.

The building closed at nine o'clock. At that time, she had left the rest room and headed down the hall. She should have had the floor to herself. The janitors normally kept to a solid routine which she had memorized after a couple nights of observation. Unfortunately, a male voice coming from around a corner had forced her to take cover in a broom closet. The voice turned out to be a security guard who was escorting a late working secretary to the elevator. Determined to get a date with the young office worker, the guard spent over ten minutes making time with her at the elevators. Domino Lady was quite relieved when the girl finally agreed to a date and left for the lobby. The annoying guard then made a tour of the floor checking for unlocked office doors. Finally, he was gone.

It was almost a relief when the Domino Lady finally made it to the door with *Havelock Investments* painted on it. She had her lockpicks out and the door open in little more than a minute. Inside, she let out a long breath. Usually this kind of job was fairly easy. It paid to remember that no job was routine, when you were a wanted woman committing felonies.

She flicked on the overhead light briefly to get her bearings. Then, back in the dark she navigated her way to the inner office door with Havelock's name on it. This lock did not take much longer that the first. Once inside this inner office she felt more secure. Flicking on the overhead light she quickly took in the layout. There was a comfortable sofa along one wall under a large painting, opposite it was a waist high wooden cabinet with glasses on its polished top. Two leather armchairs sat in front of the large desk and a padded leather swivel chair sat behind it. The window behind it showed the lights of the city spread out behind it. Most importantly, a nearly waist high steel safe stood in one far corner behind the desk. A file cabinet was in the other corner. Spotting a hooded desk lamp, she flicked the overhead light off and the desk lamp on.

She quickly searched the room. The cabinet was a bar stocked with quality liquor. She checked behind the painting to make sure there wasn't an additional hidden safe but found nothing. The desk was locked but a moment with her lock picks revealed nothing out of the ordinary. The file cabinet also contained nothing but routine business papers.

Finally, there was the safe. She had been working for months honing her skills and was confident that she could open it if she had the time. Slipping off her heels and cloak the Domino Lady got down in a comfortable position on the floor and set to work. She tried hard to remember every trick that Fitz had taught her. She closed her eyes and used just her sense of touch. The work went slowly. Her fingers grew slick with sweat as did her forehead. She wiped it with her forearm and then her fingers and arm on her long white dress. Eventually the safe gave up the first number. Then the second number. She took a brief break stretching and wiggling her fingers before continuing.

When she slowly turned the dial over the final number and felt the tumblers click gently into place, she was almost surprised. Holding her breath, she turned the handle hard to the right. There was a metallic "click" and she pulled the safe open.

Glancing at her wristwatch Domino Lady mumbled, "Well, I didn't break any records, but I got it!" This last exclamation was no louder than a low-voiced conversation but she still shushed herself as she stretched her cramped fingers. Then she flashed her pencil flash into the safe.

There were several large, leather ledgers. There was also a stack of file folders and a large manila envelope. The envelope contained a new, unused passport with Havelock's photo but an unfamiliar name. There was also two thousand dollars in cash. This was probably Havelock's insurance policy if he had to make a quick exit.

The files were marked with the names of city officials and contained

She flicked the overhead light off and the desk lamp on.

biographical and personal information on everybody from the mayor to Commissioner of Public Works. Smiling cynically, she thought, "Why would a legitimate financier need that kind of information?"

Most interesting were the ledgers. They were detailed accounting information on Havelock's business dealings. They were detailed enough that Domino Lady knew they would show an interesting picture of just where Havelock's money was coming from and going to. Unfortunately, she did not have the time or the skill to go through them tonight. Reluctantly she replaced everything in the safe.

Sitting back, she considered the one thing that was not there. This had been one of her best guesses as to where the missing necklace might be. Shaking her head, she closed the safe door and spun the combination. She stretched her back and legs and replaced her heels.

Moments later she was peeking out into the hallway; it was empty. She ducked out and quickly relocked the door behind her. She then cat-footed it down the hall around two corners and ended up in front of another office. Double checking that she had the correct suite number, she performed her magic and let herself into the darkened office. Minutes later she was easing the office window down behind her.

It was a warm night but this high there was enough breeze blowing to stir her long dress as she stood on the fire escape landing. She gave her eyes a few moments to adjust as she breathed the fresh, outside air. She then navigated her way carefully down the steep metal steps and landings until she was on the second-floor landing. Working her way carefully out onto the horizontal ladder until her weight shifted its center of gravity, she was swung gently down to the floor of the alley.

She stepped off the ladder. Free of her weight, the counter weighted ladder swung back to its horizontal position with a clang. There was no one to hear it. The Domino Lady had disappeared into the alley's shadows.

"Well, it certainly is a nice house," remarked Tony as he rang the doorbell.

"Oh, and you're going to love the Havelocks. They're such nice people," cooed Ellen as she hung on Tony's arm. Moments later the door was opened by a butler in formal livery.

Ellen spoke, "Miss Ellen Patrick and guest."

The butler nodded gravely, "You are expected, miss. This way, please."

Ellen and Tony were directed through an arch and into a large, formal living room. There several couples were sitting or standing. All had drinks in their hands. Havelock stepped forward, "Ellen, it's good of you to come." Turning to Tony, he extended his right hand, "I'm Jason Havelock. Welcome to our home."

Tony shook Havelock's hand firmly, "Tony Hulme, It's a pleasure, Mr. Havelock. Thank you for inviting us."

"Please, call me Jason."

Barbara Havelock had drifted forward in her husband's wake. She and Ellen exchanged a brief hug. Then introductions were made with the other dinner guests. The two additional couples turned out to be George Jackson, president of major Southern California bank and his wife Hilda and Martin and Deanna Whitley. Whitley was a State assemblyman representing downtown and western Los Angeles.

Introductions made, Tony and Ellen were offered drinks and the mingling began. Whitley was a good-looking young man who had a pleasant look plastered on his face. The same expression every politician Ellen had ever met used for shaking hands and politicking for votes. He quickly addressed her, "Ellen Patrick? You wouldn't be related to Owen Patrick, would you?"

Ellen smiled tightly, "I am his daughter."

Whitley's face showed surprise, "I had the honor of meeting your father a few years ago. We never worked together as I was just a legislative aide at that time but I know how respected he was. His death was a terrible blow."

Ellen worked to keep her face from showing the pain she felt at the mention of her slain father, "Thank you Mr. Whitley. It has been a very hard time for me but I am finally able to move on after those terrible events."

"His death was a great loss for the entire state. It's terrible that the authorities have never solved his murder. It's a stain on our state that a man such as your father can be murdered and his killers go unpunished."

Ellen's murdered farther was never far from her mind so Whitley did not bring up any bad memories with his solicitous words. Just the opposite, it always gave her a warm feeling when she met friends or admirers of her father. It was plain that Whitley was trying to win Ellen over. Politicians were always campaigning for votes. She had met many like him. Their endless quest for re-election money was a main source of corruption and graft in her beloved California.

Ellen smiled as she replied, "I'm sure that my father will be avenged. Justice takes strange forms. Sometimes it happens in court rooms;

sometimes it comes from sources you never expect."

Unsure how to reply to this rather cryptic remark, Whitley hesitated. He was saved by the butler entering the room and announcing dinner. Tony drifted up and Ellen took his arm as Havelock led them through the hall and into a very large, high ceilinged room. A table that would easily seat twice their number dominated the room.

The four couples took their places around the table. Tony seated Ellen and sat next to her. She found herself just opposite Mrs. Jackson. Havelock took a place at the head of the table while his wife sat at the foot. Havelock picked up his full wine glass and raised it, "Ladies and gentlemen, I thank you for coming and brightening Barbara's and my evening." Ellen joined everyone else in raising her glass as servants brought in the first course of their meal.

As expected, the wine was excellent, as was the dinner that followed. During the entrée Mrs. Jackson spoke to Ellen, "I understand you're the daughter of the late Owen Patrick, Ellen."

"Yes, I have that honor, Mrs. Jackson."

"Oh, call me Hilda, dear. It was a terrible thing the loss of your father." She glanced at Ellen's finger and then at Tony, "You're not married, are you?"

Tony felt his face flush as he sipped his wine. Ellen smiled demurely, "Oh, no. I'm not ready to settle down. I have much to do before I get serious about a family."

"Really," Hilda Jackson looked surprised. "You don't have a uh—career, do you?"

Ellen laughed pleasantly, "Oh heavens no, I'm much too busy helping my friends and raising money for charities."

Hilda smiled, "Why, that's wonderful A young lady like yourself doing such noble work. How do you go about raising money?"

Cutting her steak, Ellen shrugged casually, "Oh, I get most of my donations from individuals. Quietly, of course. Most people I deal with end up donating anonymously."

Barbara Havelock put in, "I've told Ellen that Jason and I would be glad to contribute."

"As would I. What charities do you work with, Ellen?"

"Oh, any number of ones. I have lists and send them anonymous donations when I've collected a significant amount."

"I must say that is laudable for a young person to be so interested in civic duty."

Ellen looked at her squarely, "I do it for my father, Hilda." There were nods around the table and Tony leaned in close to whisper, "Good for you, Ellen." Soon talk turned to other topics. Ellen was glad. She did give generously, and anonymously, to charities but as her masked alter ego and she preferred to keep it that way.

After dessert, the group adjourned to the living room for more drinks. Envious remarks about the Havelock mansion were made and soon Barbara was leading the other two women off on a tour. Tony and Whitley quickly surrounded Jackson and began sounding him out on politics. Havelock stood nearby listening closely. Seeing an opportunity Ellen drifted up to him, "Jason, I've seen most of the house but I hear you have a lovely swimming pool. Would it be too much to ask you to show it to me?"

Havelock raised an eyebrow. Then obviously deciding that there were worse things than showing his lovely guest the pool by moonlight, he smiled and said, "Why of course, Ellen. Come this way."

He led her through an arch, down a hallway and around a corner to a part of the mansion she had not visited before. Ellen remarked, "I've never been in this part of the house. What's that room?" She pointed. Havelock stopped and indicated closed doors nearly opposite each other, "That is the billiard room and that one is my private study." Ellen nodded and took his arm, "This is such a lovely home."

Havelock smiled down at her, "Why thank you, my dear. Uh, here we are." At the end of this short hall was a single French door leading outside. He opened it and led the way onto an expansive patio. They stood near the far end in a relatively shadowed part of it. Expensive outdoor furniture was scattered about facing a very large in ground pool. The waning moon was still nearly full and a slight breeze cooling the day's heat stirred the surface of the pool.

"Why Jason, it's beautiful here."

"Yes, Barbara loves to swim here. Too bad you didn't bring a suit. You could go for a swim."

"Oh, that wouldn't be appropriate tonight—but, perhaps I could come back some time during the day for a swim." As she said this Ellen, squeezed his arm. This pleasant thought made Havelock smile, "That would be nice."

Seeing the opening she had been waiting for Ellen leaned and spoke quietly, "Is there a place where we can talk privately—perhaps in your study, Jason?"

Looking down he whispered, Of course," and led the way back into the house. Down the short hallway he unlocked one of the two doors they had passed and ushered her in.

It was much as Ellen had imagined: a large room with a wall of books, expensive furniture, paintings on the walls and a huge hardwood desk. Moving toward a cabinet Havelock asked, "Another drink?"

Ellen crossed the oriental rug toward the desk scanning the walls as she went, "Gin and tonic, if you have it." Havelock spoke over his shoulder as he bent to open the doors of the cabinet, "Of course."

With his back turned Ellen leaned toward a painting, then quickly moved on to another. When Havelock turned back a minute later, she was staring up at a bright colored painting. He walked toward her holding out a glass of ice and liquid. Ellen took the glass and looked knowingly at him, "That's a *Cassatt*, and I'm sure it must be an original!"

Havelock looked surprised, "Why yes, it is. You are familiar with the Impressionists?"

"Oh, I took several art history and appreciation classes when I was at Berkeley."

"Yes, well I've had that a long time. It's turned out to be a good investment; worth a good bit more than I paid for it. Of course, paintings are a long-term investment. You just can't sell a painting overnight." Havelock moved closer, "What did you want to talk about, my dear?"

Ellen tried to look innocent as she spoke, "Well, you know since I don't work, I have lots of free time for my friends. Uh, I was wondering if perhaps we, that is you and I, could have lunch some time?"

Havelock was surprised. He hesitated for a moment then asked, "Aren't you and your friend Tony, uh—serious?"

Ellen laughed and shook her beautiful, blonde head of hair, "Oh, Tony is nice—and lots of fun but he's so—young. I actually prefer more mature, worldly men." She stared upward at Havelock with what she hoped was worshipful look. Havelock immediately took the bait. He smiled indulgently and replied, "I would love to have lunch sometime. We could meet downtown, perhaps at my club. Where do you live?"

Ellen sipped her drink and said. "In Hollywood, on Wilshire."

Havelock nodded, "That's very convenient. Why don't I give you my private office number?"

Another sip, "That would be nice, Jason."

Havelock turned toward the desk. Opening a drawer, he took out a pad of paper, plucked a fountain pen from its marble mount and turned to write. As he did, Ellen stepped quickly forward and touched the painting's frame. It was solidly mounted very close to the wall and did not move. By the time Havelock turned back holding out a folded square of paper, Ellen was back where she had been, finishing her drink.

Ellen took it and without looking at it slid it inside the cleavage of her dress, pressing it down between her breasts until it could not be seen, "Thank you, Jason. I'll call soon." Havelock watched, trying hard not to lick his lips in anticipation. He replied huskily, "I look forward to your call."

Ellen touched his arm and said, "Perhaps we should get back before we're missed."

"Of course, you're right," Ellen led the way out with Havelock just behind her turning off the light and relocking the door.

Moments later they were back in the living room where the three men were still talking politics. Ellen mentally shook her head thinking, "Men! They probably didn't miss us at all." The ladies soon returned chattering about paint colors and decorators. Ellen joined in making small talk. She had found out what she had come for.

Later, on the trip back to her apartment Ellen asked, "Did you have a good time?"

Tony replied, "I did. It never hurts to get acquainted with influential people. Remember, I may be needing political support myself, one day."

Ellen leaned on his shoulder, "Of course, you're going to be DA someday.""

"Well, I hope so. Can I count on your vote?"

Ellen closed her eyes, "Oh, yes!"

Five nights later Ellen sat in her roadster with the top up. It was parked fifty yards down the street from the Havelock house. She had watched the house every night since the dinner party waiting for an opportunity. Now it looked like her patience was paying off. The chauffeur had brought Havelock's DeSoto around to the front of the house and waited inside it, motor running. A few minutes later Havelock and his wife, wearing evening formal clothes, came out of the house, got in the car and were driven away.

Glancing at her watch Ellen saw it was twenty minutes to eight. She settled back down. Forty minutes later the maid and cook left together. They walked downhill on the other side of the street from her roadster. No doubt heading toward the nearest bus stop two blocks away. This all was routine. The last four nights they had left by eight thirty leaving only the

Havelocks and their muscle in the house overnight. Now she was sure the house was empty.

Tonight, Ellen was wearing a long black, backless gown. She slipped the black mask over her head and adjusted it across her nose. The Domino Lady had appeared in the back seat of the roadster. Checking the inside of her thighs to see that her small automatic pistol and syringes were snugly in place she picked up her reversible cloak and wrapped it around her shoulders, black side out. A quick look around to be sure the street was empty of passersby and she got out of the car easing the door closed silently.

The Domino Lady pulled the cloak tightly about her and drifted across the sidewalk into the shadow of large tree. This was a neighborhood of large homes set well back from the street. Large landscaped grounds were the norm. Most people here tended to stay at home minding their own business. A quick nod and the Domino Lady ghosted up the street staying in the shadows of trees as she went. The moon was waning but still half full and threw a good amount of light in open areas. It also made for deep shadows which the Lady used to her advantage.

Reaching the five-foot wall that surrounded the Havelock property presented no challenge. She boosted herself up onto it and sitting swung her legs around to the inside and jumped down lightly. With more cover from the street and neighbors she moved more confidently. She quickly made her way around the side of the darkened house until she faced the pool and patio. The patio-furniture stood out starkly in the moonlight.

At the far side of the patio she, she pulled a lock pick from her small wrist bag and set to work on the isolated French door. Three minutes later she was easing the door closed behind her. It was the work of a moment to reach the study door. It was locked as she expected, but soon yielded to her trusty lock pick. Soon she was inside the study leaning against the door.

Deciding there was too much of a chance of the room light being seen, she pulled out her pencil flash and crossed the room to the painting she had marveled over Saturday night. It was a large painting nearly two feet wide and three feet high. She pulled on the right side but it did not move. Nodding, she pulled on the left side. There was the slight resistance of a magnet pulling loose and the painting swung outward on the piano hinge mounted along its right side. Now revealed in the light of the flash was a good-sized wall safe. She smiled.

Knowing that she would be here for a while Domino Lady took off her cloak and draped it over the end of a nearby leather sofa. Turning off the light she took a deep breath and reached for the safe dial. It was slow work.

Straining her senses, she turned and re-turned the dial feeling for the tumblers. After what seemed like an eternity, she felt the first one fall into place. Encouraged she soldiered on. Minutes later the second "metallic click" was felt. Drying her fingers on her dress she resisted the urge to look at her watch. She wasn't worried about time. The Havelock's had been dressed for some kind of formal gathering. They would not be home for hours.

Back to work, she slowly turned the combination lock feeling the tiny movement through the dial. She was beginning to recognize the feel of this lock and surprisingly soon the last tumbler fell into place. Surprised, Domino Lady grasped the handle and gave it a quick turn. It opened outward.

Picking up her pencil flash she directed its narrow beam into the open safe. The first thing she saw was the butt of a revolver at the front of the safe. No doubt Havelock kept it there in case he was ever forced to open the safe by an intruder. She picked up the snub-nosed gun and shined her light on the revolving chamber. Bright brass cartridges caught the light. She set it aside on the desk and went back to the safe. There was a stack of paperwork she carted over to the desk and quickly leafed though. Wills, documents and assorted personal papers but nothing to tempt her. Back to in the safe her light caught a stack of bank banded cash. Now this was interesting. She pulled the money out and quickly counted it. There was over twenty thousand dollars in small bills, mostly tens and twenties.

Reluctantly setting down the cash Domino Lady once more turned to the safe. There was only one thing left: a blue velvet case about six inches wide by eight inches long and an inch deep. Holding her breath, she opened the obvious necklace case. It was empty.

Biting back her frustration, Domino Lady resisted the urge to hurl the case across the room. Instead she stood there for a moment bitterly disappointed. With Havelock's office safe already eliminated, she was not sure where to search next. She had been sure that she would find the necklace here.

What did the case indicate? Had the necklace been here at one time? Maybe; but where was it now? Domino Lady thought of the formally dress ed Havelocks leaving for a night out. Barbara Havelock surely would not dare to wear the necklace in public. If it was seen, the insurance company would be up in arms and be yelling "Fraud!" to anyone who would listen. No, she would have to look elsewhere. But where? With a quick glance at her watch, she muttered an oath and began replacing all the items in the safe just as they had been. She hesitated over the cash, thinking of all the good it could do but finally replaced it as well. She couldn't give away her presence yet.

Slipping on her cloak, she flashed the light quickly around. There must be no sign she had been here. The room looked just as it did when she had arrived. A moment later she was in the hall relocking the study door. She turned and walked to the end of the hallway and left through the French door, relocking it as she went.

Wrapping her cloak around her Domino Lady slid through the shadows of the yard toward the street. Reaching her car, she piled her mask and cloak in the seat next to her and started the car. No one saw her go as the car purred down the street into the night.

Later that night, Ellen sat at her dining room table sipping a drink. In her hand was a list of all the properties owned by Havelock in southern California. At least all the ones she could locate. She had visited all of them. Two were small office buildings that were occupied by legitimate businesses. Not likely he would hide something there. She had searched his offices. The only other thing he owned was an empty shoe factory in East Los Angeles. She had searched that as well. Nothing but rusty machinery and dust. It had been closed since the crash, years ago.

She got up from the table and walked across her living room to the balcony. The doors were open to let the night air cool the apartment. She leaned on the railing looking out over Wilshire Blvd. Even at this time of night the busy Hollywood thoroughfare was crowded with traffic. Her brow furrowed in thought as she sipped; the alcohol harsh in her throat. Havelock was unlikely to leave such a valuable and incriminating item as the necklace with a trusted associate or even his lawyer. It must be hidden somewhere—but where?

Perhaps it was somewhere else in the house, hidden in a wall or a hollowed-out book in the library or—it could be anywhere. As for the other locations she had searched them all—or had she. She tapped the edge of her glass softly against her lower front teeth—who was to say that the list of properties she had collected was all there was. Havelock might very well have other properties. Some place he never went and no one knew he owned.

Slipping on her cloak, she flashed the light quickly around.

Ellen smiled and swallowed the last of her gin. She knew where she was going tomorrow.

It was Friday two days later. Ellen parked her car along Spring Street and walked two blocks north toward City Hall. The towering building gleamed bright white in the late summer light. She marveled at its classic lines and gray pyramid top as she neared it. Once inside the busy lobby she took an elevator directly to the floor she had carefully scouted the day before. The operator let her out and she waited until the doors closed before walking to the office with *City Assessor's Office* painted the frosted glass upper half of the door. Before opening the office door, she checked her watch. It was eleven fifty-seven; perfect timing.

Stepping into the office Ellen was confronted by a waist high counter and a squad of office workers at their desks behind it. As she entered a woman stepped to the counter and asked, "May I help you?"

Ellen gave the woman her best smile, "Why yes, I'd like to find the owner of a certain property."

The woman returned Ellen's smile and handed her a form from a stack on the counter, "You've come to the right place. Fill out this form with the property address and we'll be glad to look it up for you." Ellen picked up the form, while covertly scanning the room. The woman looked up at the wall, "Although, we're about to close for lunch. It might be better if you fill out the form and bring it back after lunch."

Ellen folded the form and put it in her purse, "Of course. How long is lunch?"

"We'll re-open at twelve thirty."

Turning away Ellen said, "Fine. I'll be back then." She stepped through the door and went out into the corridor. Once there, she turned to her right and went down the hall to the ladies' room. Closing herself in one of the stalls she waited patiently. Almost immediately there was a rush of women entering, then came the chatter of voices, the sounds of toilets flushing, water running and stall doors opening and closing. For five minutes things were very busy then silence descended on the restroom.

Ellen exited the stall and left the restroom. The corridor was empty. She made her way back to the Assessor's Office with her lock pick in hand. Looking both ways to make she was alone, she set to work on the door's lock. A minute later she stepped into the office and relocked it behind her. She pushed through the waist high swinging door and looked around the office. Ignoring the address files and oversize plat maps she headed directly for the tax file cabinets.

Ellen had scouted the floor the day before and knew that the office emptied quickly at noon and it and the whole floor would be deserted for half an hour. Glancing at her watch she pulled a pad of paper and a pencil from her purse and went to work. Twelve minutes later she was scribbling an address down on the pad. She nodded to herself; she had overlooked one of Havelock's properties. She now had an address that no one she had talked to connected with the financier. Closing the file drawer, she moved quickly back through the office. A quick look showed her the corridor was deserted. She exited and quickly relocked the door. Moments later she entered the elevator telling the operator, "Lobby, please."

As Ellen crossed the imposing lobby, streams of mainly female office workers were streaming through into it. She glanced at her watch with a pleased look on her face; twelve twenty-eight. Pushing through the front doors onto Street Ellen turned toward her roadster thinking to herself, "Well, a fine morning's work. I think this deserves a fine lunch to match. I wonder how busy the *Formosa* is today?"

That night the Domino Lady drifted away from the roadster down a deserted street in Culver City. She soon turned into a narrow, darkened alley. The address she had acquired at the Assessor's office had led her to a closed and empty dress shop in a once thriving neighborhood. Many businesses were closed in this area. Most were to be torn down soon and replaced with a new aircraft factory reputedly owned by Howard Hughes, the movie producer. She had scouted the store that afternoon. It was located between a haberdasher and a stationary store with a *Going out of Business* sign in the window. Glancing through the dusty glass window she had seen nothing but a few abandoned dress forms and a broken mannequin lying on the dust covered floor. She speculated that Havelock must have bought it up after the crash when so many small businesses had gone bankrupt.

Now she was in the alley behind the shop looking for the back door. She soon found it. Working in the dark by feel she soon had the door open and slipped inside. Whatever room she was in did not seem to have any windows and was pitch dark. Chancing a light, she turned her pencil flashlight on and swung the narrow beam around. There was a door to a small bathroom hanging half open. Another door led presumably to the front of the shop. The only furniture was a broken chair lying in front of an old-fashioned roll top desk and—a solid looking safe in the corner beyond the desk. Checking her excitement, Domino Lady swept her light around the dusty floor. The dust was thick and undisturbed except by a set of recent footsteps leading from the back door to the safe and a superimposed set of prints leading back to the door.

She smiled in the dark as she approached the safe. The dust in front of it was disturbed. The safe itself was fairly new and when she swiped a finger across the waist high top it came away with only a light touch of dust. It had not been here for very long, perhaps only a few weeks.

Setting her flashlight down on top of the safe but pointed away, she set to work on the safe's combination. This safe was a similar model to one Fitz had had her work on and she felt confident as she closed her eyes and turned the dial. The silence was broken only by her breathing as she worked silently in the dimly lit room. It was still hard work but her familiarity with a similar model and her growing skills made the work go faster. In little more than ten minutes the last tumbler fell into place and the safe opened.

The masked woman held her breath as she pointed the flashlight into the open safe. It was totally empty except for one small object. Reaching in she pulled out a small cloth bag. Whatever was inside was heavy and felt like loose items. She set down the flashlight and, in its light, she pulled open the drawstrings that held the bag closed. Upending it, she poured the contents into her palm. The light reflected off gold and glittering gems. She wrapped it around three fingers and held it directly in the flashlight's beam. It was an intricate gold necklace set with a cascade of diamonds accenting on large center diamond. Small rubies were set at intervals adding a splash of dazzling color. Domino Lady smiled as she held the necklace and wondered how it would look set against her flawless skin and her splendid white gown.

Remembering where she was, the masked woman quickly slipped the necklace back into the cloth bag. She then closed and relocked the safe. Stepping only in the previous foot prints she made her way carefully back to the rear door. In the alley, she quickly relocked the door and walked carefully back to her car. The street still deserted, no one saw her start the roadster and drive casually away.

Back in her Hollywood apartment, Ellen walked straight to the bathroom. There she started water in the bath tub, set the temperature and added bubbling bath oil. Satisfied, she headed for her bedroom. She dropped her cloak to puddle at her feet. The white dress quickly followed. She divested herself of her compact holster and automatic as well as the twin syringes strapped to her shapely thighs. Next went her stockings and lacy underwear.

She picked up the small cloth bag and emptied the necklace into her palm. It felt cool in her hands. Holding the necklace up to the light, the diamonds and rubies glittered coldly. Stepping to the full-length mirror mounted behind her bedroom door she reached behind her neck and fastened the clasp behind her neck and under her long blonde hair. The golden links were cool against her skin. She straightened the arc of gems so they rested smoothly down her décolletage, the largest and lowest diamond nestled between her full breasts. Ellen admired the beautiful, glittering array against her flawless skin. Murmuring, "Diamonds are The Lady's best friend," she turned to admire her lush figure in profile.

She walked regally across the room to her closet. There she selected a dark blue, floor length, silk robe and wrapped it around herself. She left the bedroom and on her way to the kitchen stopped and turned off the water in the bath tub. Humming "It's Only a Paper Moon" from the Broadway play, she continued to the kitchen. From an upper cabinet she plucked a stemmed glass. From the refrigerator she pulled out a sealed bottle. It was the work of a minute to unwrap the covering and unwind the wire. A twist and the cork flew upward with a loud "Pop!" hitting the ceiling and rebounding into the sink.

The bottle in one hand and the glass in the other, Ellen glided through the apartment to the bathroom. She set the glass on the edge of the tub and poured it full of bubbling liquid. She then set the bottle down next to the side of the tub. She unbelted the robe and let it slide off her shoulders to the floor. Stepping into the tub she turned and eased herself down into the warm water with a long sigh.

Picking up the glass, Ellen sipped the chilled champagne and considered her next move. Finding the necklace was just the first part of her plan. The more important part was deciding how to use it against Havelock. She could give it anonymously to the insurance company or police but with nothing but an accusation it would be nearly meaningless. Oh, Havelock would no doubt have to reimburse the insurance company for its return. And if he had cash flow problems as she suspected, he might be in a bind with his secret backers. But what she really wanted was to expose and put a stop to Havelock's operation. She wanted to see him behind bars, not aiding and supporting crooked men and their corruption.

The best way was to arrange to have Havelock caught with the necklace. This would implicate him with large scale fraud. With him charged and in jail, a full investigation of his businesses would expose his crimes. She could replace the necklace and tip off the police that Havelock had it stashed at one of his properties. Or better yet, plant it in his office or home. But that wasn't good enough. She needed something so incriminating that there would be no way for him and his expensive lawyers to excuse his way out of.

Reaching down for the nearly full bottle, Ellen refilled her glass. She then lifted it to her full lips with her right hand while her left hand played with the necklace, rubbing it softly against her wet, slippery skin. Perhaps it was the relaxing warmth of the bubbly water, perhaps the champagne bubbles tickling her nose or maybe it was her fingers rubbing over the jewels at her throat but suddenly an inspiration popped into Ellen's mind. It was perfect. It would leave Havelock in a spotlight, caught red handed with no defense possible. It would take just the right circumstance and would require some careful planning and perfect timing but it was doable.

Ellen realized her glass was again empty and reached for the bottle. As she refilled it, she sighed because unfortunately the first step of her plan called for her to return the necklace to where she had taken it from. Still there was no hurry. She ran her fingers along the gold chain. The necklace was just fine where it was for a day or so. She smiled and sipped. She then closed her eyes, her head back against the tub and began to hum softly as she planned.

A few days later, Ellen called the number that Havelock had given her. He answered after two rings, "Hello."

Ellen replied, "Jason, this is Ellen Patrick."

There was some surprise in his voice as Havelock said, "Ellen? I was wondering if I'd hear from you."

Ellen playfully teased, "Well, of course you were. It's only been a few days. But—am I disturbing you. You must be awfully busy."

"Uh no. I can always find time for a beautiful woman."

Ellen smiled cynically to herself thinking, "If only your wife could hear you now." Aloud she shyly replied, "You're very flattering. I have been thinking of you a lot since the dinner party. Do you think we can find time to—uh, meet sometime soon?"

Havelock did not hesitate, "Of course; How about lunch tomorrow. I know a very discreet place."

Pleased he had taken the bait Ellen gushed, "Oh, that would be wonderful. Where did you have in mind?"

"Have you heard of a place called *Franconi's*?"

"No, where is it?"

Havelock named an address and added, "It's out of the way and very discreet. Despite the name, it specializes in French food rather than Italian."

"I can find it."

"Good. Can you meet me there at one tomorrow?"

"Of course."

Havelock added, "I'll describe you for the head waiter. He'll help you."

"I can't wait, Jason. See you then."

"Until tomorrow then."

After hanging up Ellen thought, "He's almost too easy. I'll have to be careful to not let things get out of hand."

The next day promptly at one o'clock, Ellen pulled her roadster over to the curb just down the street from *Franconi's*. Getting out of the car she smoothed the maroon dress she was wearing and adjusted the brim of her wide brimmed floppy hat. The expensive dress combined with the heady perfume she had dabbed behind her ears and in her cleavage should give her a potent weapon to manipulate her chosen target.

Entering the small vestibule of the restaurant she was immediately approached by a tuxedo clad head waiter. He smiled charmingly and stated, "You can only be Miss Patrick." When Ellen nodded, he smiled and led the way into the restaurant, "This way, please."

The main dining room was surprisingly small. A few tables were scattered across the floor but were unoccupied. A series of deep, shadowy booths line the right wall. All were occupied by couples sitting very close together, deep in conversation. The waiter led the way to the back of the restaurant and through a curtained doorway. Beyond was a series of doors lining both sides of the hallway. He led her to the third door on the left and knocked briefly before opening it and announcing, "Your guest has arrived, sir." He held the door open for Ellen, who slipped past him into the intimate, private dining room.

Havelock stood from the far side of a linen clad table set for two. The concealed lights were dim and there were lit candles on the table. Havelock came around the table and held out his hand, "Ellen, thank you for coming."

Ellen reached out with her hand. Havelock took her hand and brought it to his lips. Ellen, slightly surprised snuck a quick glance at the waiter but he had his back discreetly turned and was opening a bottle of champagne in a bucket near the table. Ellen summoned up her best smile and replied, "Thank you, Jason. It's good to see you again."

Havelock pulled out her chair and seated Ellen before going back to his own side of the table. Meanwhile the waiter was pouring champagne into two glasses. When finished he spoke, "Take your time ordering. Your waiter will be nearby."

Ellen picked up the menu in front of her and marveled, "This is quite a place."

Havelock nodded as he picked up his glass, "It's very exclusive. Most people have never heard of it. The chef is wonderful and the staff very discreet. More than a few important men come here for the privacy and atmosphere." Ellen tried hard not to sneer sarcastically. She could imagine rich men bringing their mistresses here. She knew the prices must be astronomical. However, the rich and powerful were used to taking what they wanted and paying through the nose for what they couldn't take.

Havelock raised his glass in a toast, "To our budding relationship."

Ellen picked up her glass and raised it in return, "To us. I've wanted to get to know you better for a while now."

Havelock's smug smile grated on Ellen's nerves but she kept a pleasant smile pasted on her face. She had to keep him interested. Sipping her champagne as she perused the menu and said, "The menu is impressive. Hmmm, the veal sounds good."

Havelock agreed, "It is very good. I think I'll have the grilled halibut." He set down the menu before continuing, "I like sea food. The chef here is good with fish but you should have the sea food at my club. It's a specialty of our chef."

"Oh, what club is that?"

Just then the waiter returned to take their orders. When they were again alone Havelock continued, "*The Sequoia Club.*"

"To us. I've wanted to get to know you better for a while now."

Ellen did not have to fake her surprise, "Really? That's impressive. I hear they're very exclusive."

Havelock nodded modestly, "Membership is restricted. We take only the wealthiest and most influential men of California for our membership."

Ellen was impressed. *The Sequoia Club of Southern California* was a very exclusive, private club of the very rich. More than one of the men she had tangled with in the last few years had belonged to it. She had several times tried to find out more about it and its membership but had been frustrated in every attempt. There were multiple reasons for this, not the least of which was; "Is it true that women are not allowed in the club, even as guests or employees?"

Havelock refilled Ellen's glass from the bottle in the ice bucket before answering, "That's true. All of our staff is male. And women guests are not allowed. This allows members to maintain privacy for business discussions and other discreet activities."

Ellen could imagine the activities that went on there, "Do you know a Gordon Richardson?"

Havelock's smile disappeared and he asked sharply, "Do you know Richardson?"

Deciding that Havelock must be a little jealous, she quickly allayed his suspicions, "Oh, not really. I met Gordon at a party last year and someone said he belonged to *The Sequoia Club*." In reality, Ellen had been studying Richardson for some time. He was a very rich man she suspected of buying public officials to support his businesses.

"Yes, I know Richardson, although not well. He's big into oil, real estate and shipping."

"That's fascinating. There must be many important men in the club. It's too bad I can't visit it."

"It's quite a place. Did you know there are private rooms and in fact whole suites upstairs for members to stay over if they choose?" Havelock raised an eyebrow and looked appraisingly at Ellen, "For special situations, exceptions can be made to the visitor rule. That is, if extreme discreetness is needed." He ended this surprising statement with thinly disguised lust in his eyes.

Ellen played innocent, "I'm sure you're very discreet, Jason."

Further exploration of this topic was interrupted by the waiter bringing their orders. The rest of their meal was filled with flirting. Soon Havelock glanced at his watch and frowned, "I'm afraid I have to go; an important meeting."

Ellen smiled, "I'm sure we'll see each other again soon."

Havelock stood up," Yes, perhaps we can have lunch again in a week or so. Oh, and we're having a party a week from this Saturday at the house. If you attend though, you should bring a date. We can find time to talk privately but we must keep up appearances.

Ellen agreed, "Of course, appearances are important. And, I have just the right date in mind."

"Good, I'll leave first. Good bye, Ellen."

"I'll see you soon, Jason." Havelock left and moments later the waiter reappeared, "The check has been taken care of, miss. Is there anything else I may bring you?"

Ellen sat back down and nodded, "Some more champagne, please." To herself she thought, "After all, Havelock is paying for it."

"Very good, miss." When the waiter had left Ellen looked thoughtful. A big party in a week would work out just about perfectly. But there were a few details to work out.

The following weekend Ellen lay atop the cabin of the sailboat enjoying the sun on her back. She looked aft at Tony sitting in the stern of the borrowed sailboat handling the tiller lightly as he looked up at the sails, judging the wind. They were off of Long Beach heading east after a day of sailing in the 24-foot sloop. She thought he looked good in his pullover, the wind ruffling his hair. She sat up and shook her long hair. Then she hopped down into the cockpit and took a seat next to Tony. He turned and gave her a long look, "You do make that swim suit look good, Ellen."

Ellen dimpled with pleasure at the compliment, "Thanks. Hey sailor, a girl gets hungry out here in all this salt air. Are you going to take me to dinner when we get back?"

"Of course. There's this great sea food restaurant just off the pier. They have the best clams there and oysters too."

"Oysters? Who needs oysters?" she asked with a grin. She brushed her hair back and looked up at the sails, "Is the wine good there?"

"Oh yes, and they have champagne as well."

She leaned in and cuddled up against his side, "I've been meaning to ask you, there's a big party at the Havelock's and I'd like you to go with me."

Tony nodded as he slipped an arm around Ellen tanned body, "I'd love to. When is it?"

"A week from today. Everybody is going to be there."

"Okay, I'll mark it on my calendar. Although we could always go dancing instead."

Ellen laughed, "Oh, I wouldn't want to miss this party. It should be one we all remember for a long time. Now, get this tub back to the dock, I'm starved."

The day of the party soon arrived. Ellen was looking at herself in the mirror when she glanced at the clock; almost seven thirty. *Tony should be along any time*, she thought. The dress itself was a rose colored, floor length and backless with a halter neck. She smiled, turning to admire it. She couldn't detect her thigh holster or the syringe through the luxurious dress. Deciding she looked perfect, she moved to a side table and picked up her clutch purse. It was larger than usual with plenty of room. She checked and found her lock picks were easily accessible, as was a spare syringe filled with fast acting knock out serum. Her black domino mask was concealed in its hidden compartment along one side of the clutch.

She pulled out a small vial of perfume and dabbed a small amount behind her ears and on the inside of her wrists. As she replaced the vial in the clutch, the doorbell rang. She opened the door to find Tony looking smart in his black tuxedo. She smiled and opened the door wide. Tony swept past pausing to give her a quick kiss on the cheek. With the door closed he gave her an approving look, "Don't you look beautiful. And, I see you got a new dress for the occasion."

Ellen smiled modestly as she posed, with one leg slightly forward, "This old thing. It's just a working dress I wear when I need something for all occasions."

Tony laughed while Ellen gathered up her clutch purse and wrap. Tony took the wrap and stepping behind her draped it over bare shoulders. He then opened the door and Ellen led them out into the hall toward the elevator. Inside as the operator guided it downward, she remarked, "I've been looking forward to this party for weeks."

Tony took her arm as the doors opened in lobby, "I'm sure you won't be disappointed. You're the one who told me everyone important in town would be there."

"Oh yes, I'm sure tonight will be exciting." Minutes later Tony was guiding them in his car across town.

Thirty minutes later Tony was shaking Jason Havelock's hand as Ellen greeted Barbara, in the foyer, "What a lovely party. Thank you so much for inviting us."

"It's a pleasure to have you, Ellen. We'll chat later after everyone is here." She turned to greet the next arriving guests. Ellen handed her wrap and purse to a maid. She felt a slight twinge knowing what was inside the clutch but trusted to the Havelock's having honest help working for them. She and Tony then strolled toward the ballroom.

There already two dozen people there chatting and drinking. Ellen recognized two city councilmen and a state assemblyman. Sighting someone interesting she nudged Tony, "Isn't that your boss over there chatting with that tall man?"

Turning his head Tony agreed, "It certainly is. I shouldn't be surprised to see the DA. He's probably here hitting up prospective campaign contributors. I better pay my respects."

Ellen let Tony lead her across to LA County's District Attorney. Stepping up he said, "Mr. Fitts. It's a pleasure to see you outside of business hours."

The thin DA turned toward them, leaning on a cane, "Why hello, Hulme. I didn't know you'd be here tonight. And with such a stunning date."

Ellen smiled shyly as Tony introduced her. Meeting Buron Fitts was a surprise bonus. Fitts had gotten his job when the last LA County DA had been prosecuted for bribery. He had also done a brief stint as Lieutenant Governor before running for DA himself. He was on her private list of public targets as the word was out that he was for sale for the right price. A price said to be so high that only the rich could afford his brand of personal justice. As Fitts gently took her hand she spoke, "Mr. Fitts, it's a pleasure to meet you. Tony has told me so much about you."

Fitts smiled thinly as he appraised her, "I'm sorry that he hasn't told me anything about you at all." He held her hand for an extra second as he added, "You probably don't remember it but I saw you when you were visiting your father in state capital several years ago. You were still in college, I believe."

Ellen, who never forgot a face especially one who was a part of the corrupt machine that dominated state politics, feigned surprise, "Oh, I'm afraid I don't remember. Father had so many—friends in Sacramento."

"Your father's death was a tragic loss to us all. You have my sympathies."

"Thank you, Mr. Fitts. I'm glad to have finally met you.

Tony intervened at this point, "I'm sure we'll have more time to talk later, Mr. Fitts. Right now, Ellen and I need to find a drink." He took her arm. As they turned away, Fitts spoke, "It was a pleasure, Miss Patrick. I look forward to speaking to you again."

Ellen smiled as she turned away, "Yes, I'm sure we'll meet again, Mr. Fitts.

As they navigated their way to a bar set up at a table in a corner Tony remarked, "It never fails to amaze me how people seem to know you or your father wherever we go."

Ellen laughed, "It's dad. He knew everyone when he worked in the state Capitol." She sobered as Tony handed her a glass of wine, "I'm sorry you never got to meet him, Tony. He would have liked you."

"Well, I hope so, and I'm sorry I never got to meet him." Sipping their drinks, the two began to mingle. There were many wealthy and influential people at the party. Ellen knew more than a few and exchanged pleasantries as she drifted through the crowd, sometimes near Tony, sometimes apart. She nursed her wine not wanting to drink too much.

A half hour later the time had come. The Havelocks were now circulating among their guests so most people must have arrived. The ballroom was crowded as were the living room and hall. Wide French doors were open and people strolled outside on the patio around the pool. She found Tony and handed him her now empty glass. He asked, "Another?"

"Not at the moment, I need to find the powder room. I'll be back in a few minutes."

Tony looked thoughtful, "Now might be a good time to go talk to the Boss about a case I'm working on."

"Perfect," thought Ellen as she gave him a little wave and faded through the crowd. She quickly made her way back to the front hall. She found the maid and asked politely, "I need to powder my nose, could I have my purse, please."

"Of course, miss. Which one is yours?"

Ellen pointed, "The beige clutch, there."

The maid handed it to her with a smile. Ellen opened it and breathed a sigh of relief to feel the necklace nestled at the bottom. She found a quarter and gave it to the maid, "Thank you. Where are the uh . . ."

The maid smiled and said, "There's one on the left of the main hall and another past the dining room." Ellen nodded her thanks and turned away. She knew very well where the bathrooms were and she wanted neither of the ones she had been pointed to. She gradually worked her way past chatting partygoers toward the rear of the house. When she was sure no one was looking she walked quickly around a corner and made her way to the rear of the house. Soon she reached the short hallway leading to the study.

A glance showed the corridor to be empty. She quickly opened the door opposite the study and stepped into the blackness. Locating a switch near the door she flipped it revealing Havelock's billiard room. She turned the key in the lock. It was the work of seconds to set her purse on the table and unhook the clasp of the halter behind her neck. Lifting up the dress, she pulled it over her head and laid it on the table. Standing in her heels, stockings and underwear she checked her small .25 automatic in its thigh holster then pulled the syringe from where it was secured against her other inner thigh.

Setting the syringe down, she quickly turned the long, rose colored gown inside out revealing that its reverse side was a bright white in color. She lifted it over her head and let its soft folds flow down her svelte figure. She smoothed it and then lifted the halter ends and secured them behind her neck. Reaching into her purse she dug into the hidden pocket and pulled out her black domino mask, slipped it on and adjusted its fit.

Domino Lady rummaged again in her purse and pulled out a lock pick. She tucked her clutch, under her left arm. Into her left hand went the syringe, into the right the lock pick. She went to the door and flicked off the light switch. In the darkness, she took a deep breath, turned the key and eased the door open enough to stick her head into the hall. It was empty. She glided across the hall, closing the door behind her.

Her gaze flicking left and right, she quickly went to work on the lock. It yielded quickly and with a sigh of relief she slipped inside the study. Knowing her time was short; she flipped on the overhead light and hurried across the room to the painting on the far wall. She returned the lock pick to her purse and set it on the desk.

Turning to the painting, she slipped the syringe in her hand into the cleavage of her dress to free her hands. She then pulled on the painting's lower edge and it swung smoothly to one side on its hinge revealing the safe behind it. Smiling, she confidently dialed the same combination numbers she had learned from her first foray, gave the handle a quick twist and the safe opened. Everything inside looked the same. She reached into it and pulled out one, two and three bundles of new cash. She went to her purse, quickly pulled out the bejeweled necklace and replaced it with the cash.

Back at the safe she swung the door wide and carefully arranged the necklace so that part of it dangled out the front of the safe, anchored by the heavy revolver. She stepped back to survey her work. It was perfect. The painting folded all the way back against the wall and the open safe door stood out against the wall. The glittering necklace was impossible to ignore. She nodded, pleased with the effect. Without warning, she heard the hall door knob turn and the door swing open behind her.

Girard the chauffeur swallowed the last of an hors d'oeuvre and turned away from the side table. Everyone seemed to be having a fine time chatting and drinking. He wished he could have a drink—but he was on duty. Excusing himself as he squeezed past guests, he began to make the rounds of the house. He wasn't worried about intruders on a busy night like tonight but there could easily be guests who wandered into parts of the house they shouldn't. More likely there might be guests who had had too much to drink and needed assistance to their cars.

Everything seemed normal as he made his way through the ballroom, living room and down the main hall. Smiling, he eased through the crowd and out onto the patio. The evening was warm and several couples were strolling around the pool. Heading past it toward the rear of the house, he noted one couple in a steamy embrace in the deep shadow of an orange tree.

Reaching the far end of the large patio, he entered the French door leading to the rear hallway. As he reached Mr. Havelock's study, he routinely rattled the doorknob to confirm it was locked. To his surprise the knob turned. Curious, but not alarmed, he pushed the door wide and was surprised to find the overhead light on and a blonde woman in a white gown standing with her back to him. He took a step forward and was about to speak, when his attention was drawn to the far wall where Mr. Havelock's wall safe was wide open, the painting concealing it swung back against the wall. Shocked he shouted, "Who the hell are you?"

Domino Lady was frozen with shock for the briefest moment as she heard the door open behind her. Her heart raced but she remained calm. With her back turned, whoever it was could not see her mask or face. The chauffeur's challenge didn't startle her but she jerked in simulated surprise, stepped backwards toward the center of the room, reached her right hand toward her bosom and crumpled silently to the floor.

Reaching into his dinner jacket for his revolver, the chauffeur stepped forward as he shouted. The woman did not turn but jumped backwards and fell to the floor, her body on its side, turned away from him. He jerked his weapon clear and walked up to the woman, "What are you doing in here?"

When there was no immediate answer, he prodded the woman in the back with the toe of one shoe. The touch of the shoe told Domino Lady exactly where the guard was. She rolled over like lightning, her right hand swinging over and down, plunging the syringe into the lower calf of the guard. He cursed and jumped back hopping on one foot. To the masked woman's relief, he didn't squeeze off a reflexive round from his weapon. She leapt to her feet and got a two-hand grip on his gun hand.

Surprised by the stabbing pain in his leg and the woman's mask, the guard gritted his teeth against the pain as she grabbed for his gun. Confident that he could handle a woman that he outweighed by more than sixty pounds, the guard snarled and grabbed for her with his free hand. As he did, his vision blurred. His strength seemed to drain away and he staggered. She pulled forward and he lost his balance, slipping to one knee. He looked up at the woman's masked face but it blurred and his eyes closed. Unconsciousness, he fell face forward onto the expensive oriental carpet.

Domino Lady quickly stepped forward and kicked guard's revolver under the sofa. She then crossed the room to the door, closed it and turned the latch to lock it, grumbling as she did, "It's stupid mistakes like this that are going to get me caught one of these days." Deciding that the guard's body would help the effect she wanted, she left him where he lay. Quickly, she unhooked her halter and lifted her dress over her head. She shook it out, reversed it and put it back on. She took off her mask and secreted it in her purse. The larger clutch easily held the cash that she had liberated along with her other gear. Lastly, she plucked out a black business card that read, *Compliments of the Domino Lady* in white ink, and slipped it into the top drawer of the desk. It would be found eventually but she doubted anyone would suspect the infamous, masked cat burglar of replacing a stolen item.

Stepping to the door she looked around once more, approving of the scene she had set. She opened the door a crack and listened for a moment. Hearing nothing, she stepped out into the hallway, swinging the door wide open. Holding tightly to her clutch, she walked to the corner, turned and walked some way toward the front of the house. Reaching a good position, she stopped and screamed.

There was an immediate hush from the buzz of distant conversation.

Multiple foot falls could be heard and around a corner came several guests. Pointing back the way she had come Ellen yelled, "Back there!"

Men rushed toward her, a police captain in dress uniform led the way. "What is it? What's wrong," he barked at her? Ellen gasped out, "I saw a masked woman come out of a room. She saw me and ran."

By this time Tony had shouldered his way past the guests crowding the hallway. Havelock was close behind him. The captain brushed past Ellen as Tony rushed up to her, "Are you all right, Ellen?"

"I'm all right. But there was a masked burglar back there. A woman!"

Tony was startled but recovered quickly. He said, "Stay here!" then turned to closely follow Havelock who was hurrying after the captain. Others pushed forward chattering among themselves. Ellen let herself be swept along with the crowd. Moments later she was pushing through the crowd to the study's entrance. Inside the study, the captain had a hand on Havelock's chest holding him back, "Don't touch anything, Havelock."

Havelock's face was twisted in anger, "That's my safe and this is my house."

"And, this is a crime scene!"

Tony had pushed forward and was staring at the safe. He pointed, "It's a crime scene all right. Maybe more than one." There was a murmur from those guests who could see. Attention shifted from the guard's unconscious body to the safe. The captain, who was closest, turned and stared hard at the necklace hanging from the safe. Havelock tried to squeeze past him and grab it but he was stopped by the captain grabbing his hand, "Not so fast, Havelock. I told you, this is a crime scene."

"You have no right to tell me . . ." He was interrupted by a man bending over the unconscious guard, "This man's alive but he's been drugged, I think." There were more whispers from the guests. Deciding that things were going as planned, Ellen faded back through the crowd. The last thing she saw was the captain pushing Havelock away from the safe and stating loudly, "Hulme, call headquarters! Tell them to get some detectives out here right away."

Things were very busy after that. Ellen got herself another glass of wine and found a quiet seat in the living room to watch the show. The guests were busy telling each other half a dozen different versions of what they thought had happened, most of them totally exaggerated. Soon the confusion was increased as sirens sounded outside. First through the door were two uniformed officers, quickly followed by a couple of plain clothes detectives. More uniformed cops soon followed. Ellen remained calm, getting her glass refilled as needed. It wasn't long after the police arrived that guests began leaving.

Tony found her in the living room, "Ellen, there you are. I'm so sorry about all this. You must have been terribly frightened. I hate to ask, but can you tell me what you saw?"

Ellen nodded graciously, "Of course, Tony. I was looking for the ladies' room when I wandered down the wrong hallway. I turned a corner and a woman in a long, white dress and wearing a mask stepped out of a room. She saw me and turned and ran the other way out a door at the end of the hall. I was so startled I screamed, then ran to find some help. You know the rest."

Tony nodded and looked thoughtful, "Did the woman have blonde hair?"

Ellen frowned, "Yes, it was. How did you know?"

Tony smiled wryly as he murmured, "Domino Lady."

"The Domino Lady! That was her?"

"I'm guessing it was. She has some nerve pulling a job during a big party."

"Wow! What was she doing?" Ellen looked puzzled.

"I'm guessing she found out that Havelock was hiding his wife's necklace and she tried to steal it. Unfortunately, or fortunately, depending on your point of view, she must have been surprised by Havelock's bodyguard and was forced to make break for it. You must have seen her as she was fleeing."

"Oh—wait a minute. What necklace? And a bodyguard? I didn't see anyone else."

"No, I guess you wouldn't have. We found him out cold in Havelock's study, his gun under a sofa. Somehow the Domino Lady got the drop on him before he could get off a shot. That's the interesting part. I'm thinking she used drugs of some kind but—who knows?" He shrugged, "And the necklace I was talking about is the one that Havelock reported stolen last spring. It was in all the papers at the time. It's very valuable. Now, it's looking like it was never stolen at all. Havelock probably faked the robbery to collect the insurance."

Ellen looked shocked, "I think I read something about that. You mean it was all phony?"

Just then two uniformed officers and a detective walked Havelock past the living room toward the front door. He was protesting his innocence loudly and demanding his lawyer. Ellen looked at Tony and pretended surprise, "You're arresting him?"

"Not me. The police. Insurance fraud is a felony, I'm afraid."

Ellen shook her head, "What a surprise. He seemed like such a nice man."

Tony shook his head in sympathy, "I guess you just never know about people."

"No, you don't," Ellen agreed.

An hour later Ellen was sitting next to Tony as he drove her home. She cuddled up next to him in the front seat and took his arm. She giggled, "You certainly know how to show a girl a good time."

Well, it wasn't the evening we had planned but it was exciting."

"It sure was. I even got to see the Domino Lady that everyone talks about."

"You were lucky. She usually comes and goes like the wind. Every cop in the city would give a week's pay to catch her."

"Speaking of catching people, are you going to be prosecuting Jason Havelock?"

Tony shook his head, "I'm afraid not. I'm a witness, remember. Although I'll be in on the consultations and people will remember me, that's the important part."

Ellen giggled again, "I suppose you have the Domino Lady to thank for this boost to your career."

"I suppose so. Maybe we should toast her for helping my career along."

Ellen squeezed his arm, "Well, there's plenty of champagne at my place."

Tony smiled and pressed down on the accelerator.

The End

It's Good to be Back

*I*t's been a while since I wrote a Domino Lady story. Not because I didn't want to and not because I didn't have any good ideas (I have plenty more neat DL story ideas where this came from), no other reasons kept me away from the beautiful masked avenger. First, I got caught up writing some other important stuff the last year or so. My first full novel took up a lot of time; especially coming directly on the heels of my first novella with my original female avenger character.

In addition, the Gods of Publishing took a hand and delayed the third *Airship 27* Domino Lady volume for a time. With volume 3 delayed, I held onto my latest Domino Lady idea and waited for a time when it was needed.

Finally, the stars were aligned and it was time to dust off my outline and get busy. Since I came up with the idea for this story quite a while ago, I've had time to put a lot of thought into it. Part of that was returning to the original 1930s stories and re-reading them. Interestingly the original stories aren't written as thrillers or mysteries. Instead they are actually romance stories set to a background of corruption and crime. Not that Domino Lady doesn't target and take down corrupt officials and other evil doers; because she does. It's just that in the original stories there was a lot of passionate moonlight kisses and other romantic scenes. While I have shown Domino Lady as a passionate, flirty woman in my first stories, I decided that I wanted a little more of that flavor in my latest DL story.

The Domino Lady is an infiltrator, a seductress and a cat burglar. This is the way I have portrayed her and I enjoy writing her this way. It's a lot of fun finding ways for her to use her flirtatious personality and abundant physical charms to achieve her goals. In this latest story it wasn't hard to show more of her flirtatious side and still have lots of scenes where she is in costume; breaking and entering or finding ways to best her formidable male opponents.

Since I plan on writing plenty more Domino Lady stories, I added a couple of scenes that will help set things up for future adventures. *The Sequoia Club of Southern California* is a totally invented organization that I have a lot of plans for. On the other hand, Buron Fitts was a real-life LA District attorney and politician who actually did a short stint as California Lieutenant Governor. Expect to see both in future Domino Lady stories that I write.

So, it was a lot of fun writing *Diamonds are the Lady's Best Friend.* That's one reason I love writing about the sexy masked avenger. She is just so much fun to write. The stories just seem to fly off my keyboard. As usual, writing this one went fast; the more I've thought out a story the faster the writing goes. In this case it took less than a week to write this story. My main problem was cutting out a few thousand words. The original version ran long and I had to cut out a couple of those romantic scenes I was talking about earlier. Oh, well!

I'm very pleased to be included in all of *Airship 27's* Domino Lady volumes. From everything I've seen, this series is popular and I see no reason why there won't be many more volumes in the series. I plan to have a story in all of them.

I hope you enjoy this latest volume of Domino Lady's adventures. I sure enjoyed writing my story and I hope to see you in the next volume as well.

GENE MOYERS - studied European and Medieval history at the University of Oregon. He is also a U.S. Army veteran. He worked in the high tech industry for some time and is also a licensed massage therapist.

An avid military gamer and role player, his favorite game was *Daredevils* a pulp based roleplaying game set in the 1930s. His love affair with the 1930s and pulps in particular stem from his first time reading a *Shadow* novel as a boy. Although interested in writing since a teen he did not turn to serious writing until 2000.

He is the co-author of *GURPS Crusades* published by Steve Jackson Games. He has written several stories for Airship 27 including stories published in all of the *Purple Scar volumes,* all of the *Domino Lady volumes, Mystery Men and Women vol.5, The Phantom Detective vol.1, Moon Man vol. 2* and *The Legends of New Pulp Fiction.* He has also written a story published in *Alternative Air Adventures* for Pro Se Publications and one published in *I.V Frost Scientific Detective* for Moonstone Books.

When not working on various new pulp projects, he is busy writing alternate history stories or horror adventures for his occult investigator, the *Dream Master.* Gene currently lives in Beaverton Oregon with his wife and three lazy dogs.

THREE DEAD MEN

By Kelly Nolan

On the docks of Los Angeles, a trio of dock workers were sitting around a shipping crate. Each held a hand of cards and were eyeing one another with suspicion. On the shipping crate laid a pile of various amounts of dollars and coins. Usually these men would have been caught and scolded by their employer, but it was one in the morning and no one was around.

"Checkmate, losers!" One of the men screamed with joy. "I won! I won! I finally beat you Al and Jerry!" The man collected the money from the makeshift table and shoved it into his pockets.

"First of all, this is a card game, Eddie," Al replied with annoyance. "You don't say checkmate in a card game. Checkmate's only for chess. Secondly, you can stop shoving it in our faces that you won! I was going to buy some movie tickets with that money"

"Well gee, I'm sorry for bragging about it, Al. This is the first I've won any kind of card game."

Jerry, the other loser, finally spoke up, "Why were you buying tickets, Al?"

"I was buying it to try to get a date with a dame," Al said with a slight sadness in his voice.

Eddie and the Jerry's eyes widened with surprise. In unison, the two asked with a high amount of interest, "A date?"

"Yeah, a date. She's absolutely gorgeous. She's got long legs."

Eddie and Jerry leaned in closer. "Yeah?"

"Her body is like an angel's."

The two listeners leaned in even closer. "Yeah?"

"Her voice is better than any singing broad you hear on the radio or in any jazz club."

Jerry and Eddie were inches away from Al. Their ears were burning for more information about the goddess that their friend was describing. After a few seconds of letting the facts sink in, Jerry spoke, "Well, who is she?"

Al was lost in his daydreams about the beautiful girl as he answered, "Ellen Patrick."

The two listeners howled with laughter after they heard the answer. Jerry fell backwards into his chair while Eddie tried to do the same. Eddie missed and fell on the floor, but he didn't care. Al had just said the funniest thing he'd heard in years and he wouldn't trade that for a hundred dollars or even a thousand dollars. Al was shocked by his friends' reaction to his answer. Al sprung from his chair and glared at his fellow coworkers. Al tried to speak over the two's laughter, "Why are you laughing? You don't think I have a chance with her?"

Eddie tried to reply through his tears of joy and chuckles, "A chance? The way I see it, she's playing the major leagues with Babe Ruth and Joe DiMaggio while you're trying to play baseball in the backyard with a stick and a rock!"

Jerry cried out like a hyena from Eddie's crack at Al. He then added to then continued their roasting of their friend, "You'd have better luck trying to date Frances Kilgore or better yet the Domino Lady!"

Al was furious from the comments from his friends, so he pulled out a handkerchief. The small piece of cloth had the initials E.P. sown in. "Look at this, you idiots!" he screamed at them. His arm shook from the rage pumping through his veins. "This is the handkerchief of Ellen Patrick. She threw it to me from her hotel window as I passed by. Clearly that means she's heads over heels in love with me!"

Eddie chimed in, "Wow, gee. Look at that, Jerry." Eddie then made a playful jab at Jerry with his elbow. "It's my handkerchief that I dropped last week!"

Jerry couldn't stop from cracking up with Eddie. "Al, you've lost your mind! That's not Ellen Page's handkerchief. She'd never throw it to you."

Al, outraged from the joke that they were making him out to be, stormed out of the building holding the shipping crates. As he stormed out he yelled at them, "You two can burn in hell!"

Jerry wiped the tears out of his eyes and yelled out to Al, "Where are you going?"

"Out for a goddamn smoke! Not that you careless, good for nothing sons of bitches care!" Al leaned against the wooden building's wall. He pulled out a cigar and a lighter. He brought the cigar to his mouth and tried to get a small flame from his new lighter, but only sparks came from the small device. "Goddamn it."

"Need a light?" a voice asked from the darkness. Al turned to see who had made the generous offer to him but was met by a gun barrel aimed at his head. The man behind the pistol had the smile of a panther when it finds its new prey. "Here's one for you."

For only the time that it takes to blink an eye, there was light. The light from a gun barrel as a bullet found an exit from its prison only to end up in another prison that goes by the name of Al's head. Jerry and Eddie stopped laughing when they heard the loud blast of the pistol. Jerry called out, worry and concern filled his voice, "Al, you okay?"

The gunman appeared in the wide entrance of the warehouse and started nonchalantly walking towards the duo of dock workers. The armed man drew his pistol and provided an explanation, "Al is not okay. That's what happens to people with bullets in them."

Jerry and Eddie run away in opposite directions as the stranger begins to unload bullets. After three rounds were shot, a small underestimated killer pierced Eddie's back and burrowed its way through the chest. Eddie fell to the ground. He desperately tried to breathe through the newfound pain. Al's killer walked up to him and stomped his foot onto Eddie's back to hold him in place. Eddie begged for mercy through his short breaths, but the killer was deaf to the cries of the soon-to-be corpse that laid before him. The gunman raised his gun and put a bullet in the heart of the dock worker.

Jerry hid behind a crate as the killer slaughtered his friend. Jerry tried to stay quiet through his tears and panic, but ultimately failed. The death dealer followed the cries of the dock worker. It took little time for the expert to find the man, but the predator did want to lose his prey. He carefully leaned around the corner to see the position the target's head would be then slipped back to the corner he had taken. Like an expert he aimed at the wall of the crate and fired. The bullet broke through the wooden walls like a flash and hit its target. The hidden man fell at the feet of his killer. The killer smiled at his accomplishment and walked away. After his slaughter, he opened his mouth and yelled to a distant party, "The men are dead. Bring in the trucks." As trucks drove into the warehouse and men began to load them, the crate that had been shot was now leaking white liquid from its seams to the knowledge of no one in the building.

Roger McKane stopped in front of a hotel and stepped out of his black automobile. He walked past the hotel doorman and hotel clerk. He entered the elevator and told the elevator operator which floor to go to. The investigator leaned back on one of the walls of the elevator. He could finally rest and think for a few seconds. For the past few hours, his mind had been filled with a cocktail made from confusion, anger, fear, questions, worry, and so many other emotions. *Has she lied to me this entire time,* McKane thought. *No, I can't think like that. She's probably innocent.*

The elevator reached the Ellen's floor and Roger stepped out in a rush. He headed towards the door at the end of the hallway. *But on the other hand, she could have been hiding it the entire time,* the private eye thought to himself. He almost slapped himself in the face for ever having the thought pass through his mind. *No! God no! This is Ellen, she wouldn't hurt anyone.*

Roger McKane finally reached the hotel door. With a shaky hand, he knocked several times. A voice from inside called out, "Just a minute."

Roger felt a little easy from hearing the angel's voice from inside, but then another cocktail of mixed emotions was served to him. For an entire minute, the detective tried to cool himself off from the pressure of the situation. He tried to loosen up his tie. That didn't work. He tried undoing a button from his shirt, but that didn't work either. He tried taking off the jacket he was wearing and rolling up his sleeves, but nothing worked. He couldn't stop thinking about it. His mind pierced Roger's soul with another grim thought, *Could she really have done such an awful thing? What else could she have done?*

The hotel door finally opened to the relief of Roger. As the door opens, a Nordic beauty is revealed. It was Ellen Patrick dressed only in a black silk bathrobe. It stuck to her skin like a glove. Roger with wide eyes looked up and down the goddess. From her naturally tanned legs to the slightly wet blonde hair, there was no doubt about it. Ellen Patrick was a woman. A woman that could drive most men and some girls wild from just a look. Finally, the red lips of the woman spoke, "Hey Roge, I like that casual look you're aiming for. It looks great on you"

Roger blinked several times to break himself from the daze of Ellen's beauty. He finally was able to spit out some words that made up an actual English sentence, "Th–thanks, Ellen. You look great too." He froze stiff. *Did I just say that?* he thought. *Way to put my foot in my mouth.*

Ellen blushed from his compliment. "Thanks, Roge," she said with a schoolgirl smile. "I'm glad you like my little outfit. Come on in." As the detective walked in, Ellen stayed at the door with a grin on her face. She admired his physique as he walked past her. *He's such a hunk,* she thought to herself. *The way he had his shirt unbuttoned just a little. The way he barely noticed me sneak a peek at his chest. Oh, it can make a girl just melt.*

Ellen snapped out of her daydream as soon as she started it. She began to scold herself, "Now's not the time for boy toys. Keep your head straight, Ellen."

Roger turned around. "Did you say something?"

"I didn't say anything," Ellen said with a concealing smile. She closed the door and walked over to a table with various bottles filled with different kinds of alcohol. "You have a seat. I'll pour you some brandy."

Roger sat down on the couch. He placed his jacket on the table in front of him and pulled out a paper bag from one of the inside pockets. "No thank you, Ellen. I need to talk to you."

"Oh?" Ellen turned around with her eyebrows raised. "What is it?"

Roger reached into the bag and took out a bloody white cloth with the letters *E.P.* sewn in. Ellen gasped. "It's about this. The police and I went down to the docks after we got a call about three dead dock workers. According to the call and our investigation they were all shot dead. We investigated the scene and found this on one of the corpses. Some of the cops think the victim pulled it off the killer or it fell off the killer during a fight. Now, Ellen, I'm not accusing you of killing these people, but I need to know. Is this your handkerchief?"

Ellen steadied herself on the table behind her. She was shocked that she was connected to a crime like this. For the first time since her father's death, she was scared. She could go to prison for a crime that she didn't commit. Her family's good name would be destroyed. After adjusting herself from the shock, she responded with panic in her voice, "It is mine, Roger, but I didn't kill those people. I've never shot a gun in my life, let alone held one."

This was a lie, of course, since Ellen had both shot and held a gun many times in her life as The Domino Lady. It may have been a lie, but for a few moments it felt real. For a few moments she completely forgot that almost every week she carried a gun as the Domino Lady. The fear, panic, and shock made the weapon feel repulsive.

Ellen turned to the table behind her and with shaking hands drew a glass cup from a metal platter. She blindly reached for a bottle of alcohol as she looked straight down at the cup. She tried to focus on anything except reality. She knocked over several other bottles on the way to the glass bottle of brandy. As she opened and poured her glass full, the bottles rolled off the table and shattered onto the wooden floor. Roger practically leaped from his chair to Ellen's side. Roger asked with dread filling his head, "Ellen, are you okay?"

Ellen gulped the strong drink down her throat with incredible speed. John ran to her side. "Ellen! Ellen, you need to sit down."

Roger guided her to the couch. He carefully avoided the broken glass and liquids on the floor. Ellen sat down and slowly tried to drag herself back to reality. Roger took out a mop and broom from the living room's closet and cleaned up the mess while she sat there thinking, *I can't run away from this. This is different than when I was framed as the Domino Lady, I can't just stop being Ellen Patrick. There's only one thing I can do. Tell the truth about how I lost my handkerchief and find the killer as the Domino Lady.*

Roger finished cleaning up the mess and sat down beside Ellen. His hand reached and touched her silk covered shoulder. Roger tried his best to comfort his friend, "Ellen, I'm sorry that you got dragged into this mess and I'll do everything I can to keep the police from accusing you of the crime. Are you okay now?"

Ellen turned her head to Roger and expertly acted the role of the poor, helpless damsel. "I—I think so, but I could never survive jail. Oh, please don't let them throw me in there, Roge!" Ellen forced several tears to come out of her beautiful, sparkling brown eyes. She then threw herself onto the detective in an embrace. He was like putty her hands.

Roger was at first surprised by the sudden hug, but then he hugged her back. He comforted the girl with his baritone voice, "I will do everything it takes, Ellen." He then carefully separated the two of them and began to ask her some more questions. "Do you know how the handkerchief got into the hands of this dead man? I can show you an artist's reconstruction of the man's if that will help."

Ellen wiped her tears away from her gorgeous face. She placed a little desperateness in her voice as she answered, "Yes, that would help, Roge."

Roger reached into his coat from the table and pulled out a folded paper. He unfolded it and showed it to Ellen. On the piece of paper was the drawing of the dead man from the docks. "I know who he is," she tried to hide the disgust from her answer. She thought the man was a creep for what he did. "So, I had my window open on a breezy day last week and as I was getting ready for a party this man decided to try to sneak a look at me from. He called out to me from the street below. He called me toots and then he said that I should let him up to my floor to help undress. I went to the window to yell at him with my handkerchief in hand, but as I was about to yell at him I accidentally dropped my handkerchief and he went running off with it. If you don't believe me you can ask the hotel staff, I asked for one of them to help me go after him, but we couldn't find him."

Roger took out a notepad and pencil from his jacket pocket. He wrote down Ellen's statement and then put it back in his pocket. "I believe you,

Ellen, and I'm sure the police will believe you with your statement," he said while he picked up his jacket and put it on. "Don't leave town until we find the real culprit. It may look suspicious."

Ellen placed a nervous smile onto her face. "I won't go out of town. I promise," she said with a small fake quiver in her delicate voice. "Why don't you ask the Domino Lady to help you? She's helped you in the past."

Roger stood up and walked towards the hotel door. He answered, "I would if I could, but she's hard to get in touch with."

"Maybe she'll contact you."

"Maybe," he answered with the door open.

Before he could leave, Ellen called out, "Oh Roge." Roger stopped dead in his tracks. Ellen walked up to him and kissed his cheek. "Here's a little motivation for you."

Roger blushed and then left the room. The door then shut, and Ellen ran to get a pencil and paper. She wrote down a message as fast as she could and placed in an envelope. With the letter in hand, she ran to the other side of the room to get some clothes. She threw off her robe and grabbed some blue jeans, flats, a newsboy cap, and a button up shirt. She pulled the jeans over her tan legs and buttoned the shirt up to her delicate neck. She then hid her long hair in the hat. She grabbed shoes and with the speed of a cheetah, she moved to the door. She placed her ear to the door and listened while she put on the shoes and tucked the letter in the pants' back pocket.

Roger reached the elevator. The elevator operator was conveniently waiting for him. He stepped in and told the man to go down to the first floor. The elevator began to move.

Once it started, Ellen threw her hotel door open and ran down the hallway to the staircase. She dashed down the flight of stairs. She finally reached the first floor and burst through the staircase door. She couldn't see Roger anywhere. *Maybe I'm early,* she thought to herself. Ellen turned to the hotel entrance and saw Roger in his car. She rushed to the door as Roger was about to drive away.

The black car began to pull out of its parking space when the disguised Ellen jumped in front of it. Roger pushed down the brake as hard as he could. Roger stepped out and looked over the girl who had just been seconds away from being roadkill. Roger asked the girl lying on the ground as he walked over, "Oh my God! Miss, are you all right?"

While he was walking over, Ellen reached under the black car to dirty her hands. She then rubbed the mixture of dust, dirt, and grease over her face. Roger made his way around his car to check on the "victim." He reached out his hand to help her up. Ellen grabbed the detective's hand and pulled herself up. After dusting her clothes off, she answered Roger's question with the best New York accent she could muster, "I'm fine, hot stuff. You should really watch where you drive this thing." She patted the hood of the car. "Anyways, here's a letter for you. Some masked broad gave it to me to give to you. My work here's done so see you around, lover boy." She walked into the nearest alley, leaving a very confused Roger with a letter in hand.

He opened the envelope and read the mysterious contents. It read, *"Meet me at the bar near the docks tonight. From, The Domino Lady."*

At the end of the bar, a woman sat. She had golden hair and red lips. Some would say that she had the face of angel while the wiser would say that she has the face of a Valkyrie. When people think of an angel, they think of a beautiful winged figure that stands idly by singing. An angel is just a mantel piece while a Valkyrie is so much more. A Valkyrie is a beautiful winged figure who has their sword out to protect the innocent and fight with fellow warriors and that's exactly what the woman before us did. She was missing wings and a sword, but she was fine without those. What was in her possession was a gun, a syringe, a white cape, and a black dress. As we've said before, she does fine without a sword. She sipped at a cup of brandy while waiting for her new comrade.

The door to the bar opened, hitting the bell above it. In walked Roger McKane. The masked girl at the end of bar spoke, "Hello, detective."

Roger was surprised by her appearance, but quickly got over it. "Why did you call me here, Domino Lady?" Ellen couldn't help, but grin with amusement from hearing him say those words.

"To help solve a mystery."

"Have you been to the docks yet?"

"No. I was waiting for you."

Roger walked over to her and pulled up a stool next to her. He sat down and asked, "When do we start?"

The Domino Lady picked up her drink and turned around on her bar stool. After facing the complete opposite direction from where she faced before only then did she lean her back on the bar. "After I finish my drink. You can order a drink, if you want."

She sipped away at the glass and eyed the detective with a seductive glare. He didn't notice how the masked woman looked him over. "No thanks. Isn't brandy a little strong for most women?"

Ellen pulled her black dress back a little to reveal a gun and a syringe in her garter belt. The femme fatale's gun was a silver plated .22 caliber automatic and the syringe was filled with her signature fast acting knockout drug. "Do I look like a weak woman to you, McKane?" she responded.

"No, miss." He tried to go back on what he just said. "Far from it."

The final drop of the drink passed the lips of the lady in the black dress. She set the glass down on the bar and stood up from her bar stool. She leaned into Roger's ear and whispered, "Be a doll and pay the man for my drink."

She walked out the door of the bar and waited for him outside. Soon the inspector walked out as well. "Let's go," said the lady in the white cape.

The unlikely pair got into McKane's car and drove to the docks. There was no one around the streets that night except for the black car that was making its way towards its destination. After a brief five minutes, they made it to their destination. They stepped out and entered the scene of the crime. The bodies had already been moved to the city morgue, but there was still plenty of evidence. After looking over the scene, the Domino Lady spoke. "What do you think happened here?"

"Three dock workers were on nightshift and were playing a game of cards. One of them walked out and had a smoke, but then the killer attacked. He shot the smoker first, then he went in for the other dock workers. The remaining dock workers tried to flee, but they were both gunned down. One of them were found near the shipping crates in the back and the other was found to the left side of the building"

After a long silence, Ellen broke it with only a few words, "There's more to this." She walked over to something that caught her eye. It was a pair of tire tracks. She bent down to get a closer look. "Why would these be here at the murder scene?"

Roger shrugged. "Maybe that was the gunman's car. After shooting the first man, he pulled into the building and shot at the others."

"How many times was each worker shot?"

"The smoker was shot only once. The one on the left side of the building was shot twice. The last one was shot once."

"He was using a pistol. If he was driving a car, why would he use a pistol for a drive by shooting? Why would he pull into the building for a drive by shooting? All of the workers were lined up perfectly to use a machine gun

"What do you think happened here?"

to take them all down?"

As they pondered why, Roger noticed a trail of white liquid. He walked away from the masked woman and followed it straight to the source. He called out. "Domino Lady, I found something!"

Ellen walked over to the detective. She arrived, and a sharp foul smell hit her nose. It took a significant amount of strength to not throw up from the awful stench. She looked around to find the source of the terrible smell only to find a white puddle on the floor. It had been mixed with the blood from the dock worker, but the red of the blood didn't stop the white puddle from having an extremely pale color. "What is that?"

"I'm not sure, but it smells like some awfully made vinegar. I wish they let me back here earlier to investigate to see what this crap was."

Ellen's ears perked up. "Why wouldn't they let you back here? You're a detective."

"Well, they wouldn't let me back here since I'm technically a civilian. They'll let me work with them and ask questions to certain people they think might help the investigation, but that's about it. They don't think I'm a real detective."

Ellen sighed. She knew that he was as good as any other detective on the force, maybe even better. Clearly, they thought her friend was just an amateur. He wouldn't ignore a huge clue like this on the floor like they did. The Domino Lady had to put aside her personal feelings about the matter now though. She had a mystery to solve. "Where was the body laying when you saw it?"

McKane pointed at the floor in front of them. "About here," he guessed.

"Okay. Now this part is very important, where was the head and where was the head when you saw it?"

McKane walked about four feet away from the white puddle and pointed down. "About here," he said. He pointed at the center of the puddle that was five feet from where he stood. "The feet were over there."

The Domino Lady did the math in her head. She then pulled out her gun from her garter and aimed it at Roger's feet. Roger started to panic, "What are you doing?"

"Relax. I'm trying to figure something out." Ellen then made an arch in the air with the pistol. She stopped making the arch at about five feet above the ground. The barrel of the gun was now pointed at the wall.

"Oh, I get it. You found out where he was shot, didn't you?"

"That's right. It seems there was a box in the way when he shot the victim. The box was filled with bottles of this liquid. So, when it was shot, some bottles broke, and whatever this garbage is oozed out of the seams."

"The box is missing though," noted Roger. "Maybe they killed these guys to cover their tracks of importing this stuff in."

Roger took out a pocket knife and opened it. With the edge of the blade, he scooped up some of the white liquid. He kept the knife steady and pulled out a lighter. He lit the flame under the blade and saw the liquid bubble and change color. It turned from a pale white to a disgusting brown. "It's heroin," he said. "Someone must be importing this stuff and didn't want anyone at the docks to find out."

"If they're importing it," she added. "There must have been forty of fifty crates filled with heroin in here last night."

"That's why there were tire tracks on the floor. They had a team load up the crates as fast as they could. Then they drove off before anyone knew they were here."

The lady in black walked away from the puddle of blood and heroin. The detective followed closely behind. "We need to find the harbormaster," she said with determination.

"Who?"

"The man who runs the docks. He would know who ships things in and out. He would know who ordered these men to be killed."

"That's great and all, but how do we find him? We don't even know who he is."

The Domino Lady stepped into Roger's black car. With a smile and a wink, she answered, "Oh I know who he is."

Ellen knew exactly who the harbormaster of Los Angeles was. His name was Norman Johnson and he was the very definition of sleazebag. She had encountered him at several parties and every time she felt like throwing up afterwards. The way he looked at women like slabs of meat. How he tried to usher women to his excuse of a house. He even tried hitting on the mayor's wife. It was a miracle that he wasn't fired or punched yet.

"Domino," Roger interrupted her thoughts. "Where do I turn now?"

The white caped vigilante answered, "Turn left and then keep going until you see a dump."

The car was dead quiet after that. The only sounds were of the engine and the rubber tires sliding on asphalt. Roger then spoke up to make conversation, "It sounds like you have some beef with this guy."

Ellen turned to him. Her brown eyes pierced through her mask and the darkness of the night. Her red lips opened to let out her angelic voice. "Doesn't everyone?"

"Not me. I've never heard of the guy. Maybe you can put things in perspective for me and I can see what kind of person he is. Maybe he's not so bad."

"Imagine a man who's a complete slob and looks at every woman he sees as cheap objects that are willing to do his bidding," she snapped. "Then imagine a man who in his frustration of not getting laid, tries to exploit any woman who takes the time to pity him for a few seconds."

"Oh. He's that kind of guy." Rog was all too familiar with the type. "Just don't take it out on me, Okay?"

"Sorry. You're right. It's not your fault that Norman is such a jerk."

"It's fine. This is going to sound weird, but you reminded me of someone when you got riled up."

"Really," Ellen asked with a comforting smile. "Who?"

"You wouldn't know her, but her name's Ellen Patrick. She'd say the exact same thing about Johnson if she was here right now."

"Oh, does Mr. Detective have a crush on Ms. Patrick," she asked with a sly smile. "Does he want to make Ms. Patrick into Mrs. Detective?"

"I don't know if she likes me that way," Roger chuckled.

"So, you do have a crush on her."

"Well umm, I mean I wouldn't mind to umm," he shifted in his leather seat. He desperately looked for an exit from the conversation. "Oh, look there's the house."

Ellen sighed in disappointment. She desperately wanted to know how Roge felt about her, but she knew that it was a fruitless venture deep down. She couldn't be with Roge or anyone until she was through with being the Domino Lady.

Ellen and Roger both stepped out of the car. The masked blonde playfully pointed a finger at her private eye companion. "This conversation isn't over, McKane." The two walked towards the two-story white wooden house. Paint chipped away from the wood and several windows were broken. Part of the roof had caved in on the second story. The previous owner of the house had planted some flowers, but they were long dead. Behind the dead flower bed was the kitchen window. Although it was still in good condition, the objects that lied behind it were not. In the kitchen there was moldy bread and rotten fruit.

The Domino Lady and the detective entered this garbage heap that was commonly referred to as a house. With the Domino Lady leading, they walked down the hallway and the Nordic beauty drew her gun from her garter belt. McKane saw the silver piece shimmer in the moonlight and began to panic.

"What are you doing," he whispered. "We can't ask him questions if he's dead."

"Relax. It's only for protection. We have no idea if this creep is armed or not."

McKane shrugged and drew his gun from its holster as well. With pistols in hand, the two silent figures edged their way down the hallway. Suddenly a gong was struck. "What the hell was that?" the Domino Lady puzzled.

The sound of an airplane diving rang through the house. The two companions stared at each other in bewilderment. A voice began to speak, "The Skelly Oil Company presents...Captain Midnight!"

McKane's hand came to his face as realization hit him. "Oooh," he stated with a smile. "It's that kids' radio show. It's kind of dumb if you ask me."

The Domino Lady stopped in her tracks. She turned around to Roger to face him. "It's not dumb, McKane," she stated with her delicate hand on her hip. "Captain Midnight's a great guy."

"You act like you've met him."

"Actually, I have."

Roger's jaw dropped. "What? You mean to tell me he's real?"

"Yeah. We fought some criminals together a few times. He was so handsome and that wingsuit he wears leaves very little to the imagination," she said while daydreaming about Captain Midnight.

"He doesn't wear a wingsuit. He flies a plane."

"He does that too. That's one of the things that radio show left out. I guess it's because it's top secret or maybe they thought people would have a hard time believing it."

"Why does he have a radio show at all?"

"Because he's a nice guy and wants to entertain kids. When he has the time, he comes in and voices himself on the radio. He's just so dreamy."

Roger was confused. *Is she serious,* he thought. "Captain Midnight can't be real. He's just fiction on the radio, isn't he?"

Roger was pulled out of his thoughts when he felt the Domino Lady pinch his cheek. "Don't worry, McKane," she flirted. "I think you're just as cute as he is. Now let's focus."

Ellen turned around and began to walk down the hallway. She couldn't stop herself from grinning. *This is great,* she thought. *I can flirt with Roge as much as I want. I couldn't do this without the mask. Then he might suspect me to actually be interested and maybe he'd try to ask me out on a date. Although would that be so bad? Yes, it would be! I can't date him or anyone no matter how cute they are while I still go out as the Domino Lady. Now focus Ellen!*

Roger and Ellen reached the end of the hallway and came across a room. It was filled with a terrible stench, old newspapers dating back to 1929, cigar ash, empty beer bottles, a coffee table, and a couch struggling to hold the weight that rested on itself. The weight was a fat disgusting specimen known as Norman Johnson. An empty beer bottle rested on his suit. The suit, no doubt, was Norman's attempt at looking presentable to women he tried to seduce, but of course his ventures were fruitless given the lack of any perfume, lingerie, dresses, or women in the house. Beside the couch was a nightstand that propped up a shotgun.

They briefly looked at one another and nodded. The detective crept his way towards the sloth and the Domino Lady made her way towards the shotgun. Roger silently edged closer. Suddenly a crunch was heard. Roger looked down and beneath his foot was a bag of potato chips. He then looked up and saw Norman's eyes fling open.

"What the hell," Norman said groggily. His vision adjusted to the darkness and his eyes came across Roger McKane standing in his living room. The sight of a stranger in his house gave the blob of flesh a boost of energy and rage. His grogginess turned into a loud rage. "What the hell are you doing in my house?"

Ellen saw the commotion from her position and ran for the shotgun. Norman Johnson reached for the dangerous weapon. He grabbed the barrel of the shotgun and pulled it over the arm of the couch. Roger stood completely still. He wanted to try to talk to him, but he didn't realize that the man before him was a "shoot first, ask questions later" kind of person. Ellen dove at Norman as he put his finger on the trigger. Domino Lady collided into the shotgun and the aim of the weapon was pushed away from Roger. The gun went off and the spray from the shotgun implanted itself straight into the wooden wall. Domino Lady landed on the couch beside Johnson, her gun fell to the floor. With a great fury, she ripped the shotgun away from his chubby hands and stood up. Johnson looked up at her and yelled, "You stupid bi—"

Without breaking eye contact with the fat man, the Domino Lady pulled the lever down on the shotgun and fired it into the ceiling. She pulled the lever again and aimed it at him. "If you try to hurt him again," she spoke through gritted teeth. "I will unload every shell from this gun until you are a lifeless unrecognizable heap of flesh on the floor. Do you understand?"

Sweat poured down the harbormaster's face and fear filled his veins. He nodded and struggled to speak, "Y-y-yes ma'am."

"Good," she growled. Her voice changed from fury to worry as she called out. "Roger are you okay?"

"Yeah. I'm okay, Domino. That was a close one."

Domino Lady sighed with relief and her attention returned to the slob before her. "Now the detective here as a few questions he would like to ask you," she said. She pushed the end of the barrel closer to the man's neck. "I would suggest you answer his questions honestly."

Roger holstered his weapon and pulled out his pencil and notebook. He sat on the coffee table in front of Johnson and started asking questions, "Mr. Johnson, as I understand it you are the harbormaster. Is this true?"

"Yes. Yes, that's true."

"Okay. Now as you are aware, three dockworkers were murdered. Me and my colleague here are trying to find the killer. Now to find the killer we have to find out who had at least half of the building filled with their shipping crates. We know that the two are connected. Now if you would be so kind to reveal who–"

"It was Shiro Tanaka. He brought in a lot of those shipping crates."

"Are you sure?"

"I'm sure. I'm sure."

Roger wrote down the name in his notepad and looked up at the Domino Lady and smiled, "I think we just found our killer. Thank you for your time, Mr. Johnson."

"You're welcome, mister. I can help you with anything else if you want," he said nervously.

"I think that will be all," Roger said. He got off of the coffee table and walked out of the room. "Goodbye, Mr. Johnson."

The Domino Lady kneeled down to Johnson's level to face him. She still held the gun in her hand. "Norman Johnson, there are a few things I need to tell you before I leave. One, clean and fix up your house. Two, stop trying to exploit women. Three, stop being a slob. Four, turn your life around. If you fail to do any of these, I will come back, and I will teach you another lesson. Understood?"

Johnson shook his head up and down. "Yes ma'am. I promise just please don't hurt me."

Domino Lady threw the shotgun behind the couch and smiled, "Good.

Hopefully I won't be seeing you."

Domino Lady picked up her gun, placed it in her garter, and left the room. She walked down the hall and exited the house. She found Roger sitting on the car hood. "What did you tell him," he asked.

The Domino Lady climbed into the car and said, "Just to fix his life and stop exploiting women."

"Do you think it will work?"

"Who knows?"

Roger turned to her and looked past the black mask and into her brown eyes. "Thanks for saving me back there. I would have been dead if you didn't jump in there when you did."

Domino Lady turned away from his handsome stare and grinned. "It's nothing. You would have done the same thing for me. We're partners. At least, for this case."

"Yeah. I owe you one though. So how do we get into Shiro Tanaka's place wherever it is?"

"I may know a way. Expect a call tomorrow from Mr. Tanaka, that'll be your way in."

"How will you get in?"

"A magician never reveals his secrets so why should I," she said with a mischievous, taunting smile.

Ellen Patrick rolled out of bed. The night before, Roger dropped her off at the bar near the docks as the Domino Lady. When Roger drove off, she stripped herself of the Domino Lady and became Ellen once more. She had walked to her white car that was parked a block away, entered it, and threw the cape and mask into a bag. She drove to the hotel and went up to her room with the bag. She threw the bag into a chair, took off of the dress, and fell onto the bed. She slept throughout the night, but now she was awake.

She stretched her long legs as she walked over to her phone. Her delicate fingers ran themselves across the dial and soon a voice on the telephone came through. "How may I help you today?"

"Could you let me speak with Mr. Shiro Tanaka," Ellen spoke with her good girl persona shining through her voice.

"Yes ma'am. I'll patch you through."

In a Californian mansion, a man in a black suit sat in a comfortable chair behind his desk. He was a black-haired man of Japanese descent and his features at the moment were that of an angry war general, but he was not a general. At least not an official one. He waged a war of power, greed, and money in the muddy depths of the criminal underworld. He had already gained a fourth of criminal territory of his home country, but he wanted more. He wanted California. The five men in front of him had delayed his acquisition of his desired prize.

Before his desks stood his anxious employees.

"You idiots," he screamed with his mighty voice. "Do you realize what you have done?"

Most of the men shook with fear at their boss' rage. One man stared coldly at Tanaka as words fell out the employer's mouth. The fearless man couldn't bring himself to care about what the man was screaming about.

"You let a crate filled with my heroin spill and you left it there! Do you realize that if the police in this country were smarter they could have traced it back to me," he asked as he stood from the chair. He walked around the desk and passed the shaking men. Some were on the verge of tears, some were sweating from the stress, some were hyperventilating. All of the men in the room were panicking inside except for the man at the end of the line on the left. Tanaka looked up at the tall, bald man with nothing but anger. "And then there's you, American. You and your complete disregard for my product. Besides the fact that you shot a hole through one of my crates, you left behind several bodies. You were supposed to dispose of them, Mr. Cooper!"

Mr. Cooper's cold stare met with Shiro's rage filled eyes. The two stared at one another for a minute. It was truly an unstoppable force meeting an unmovable object. After a minute the hired gun spoke, "You know I usually kill men for insulting me, correct?"

Tanaka smiled a devilish smile. He spoke through the smile, "I do. It's something I can respect because I will kill anyone for failing me." Tanaka walked back to his desk. Each step made echoed through the room and filled the ears of the cowering men. Tanaka reached his desk and picked up a letter opener.

He walked over to one of the fearful men and plunged it straight into its neck. The man's face was frozen in fear as Tanaka's dragged the impromptu knife across the man's throat. Tanaka's face was frozen as well, but it was the face of a killer. As he pushed the dead man aside the other men stood in place. He looked them over one by one. He then walked behind them to get another perspective.

"And then there's you, American."

He noticed the man that the man next to the current holder of the letter opener was visibly shaken. Shiro stopped by the man on the end of the line at the right. The man was visibly shaken so Tanaka reached out his hand to the man's shoulder and rested it on it. The man jumped and screamed out in fear. The resting hand turned into a firm grip on the man's shoulder and another hand grabbed the hair of the man from the back. He screamed, "Oh God! Oh God! Not me!"

Shiro dragged the struggling man by his hair and his shoulder to his desk. He slammed the man's head into the desk. He then proceeded to do the same action to the man's head several more times. The man was still struggling so Shiro threw him over the desk. The man rolled over it and onto the floor.

The tired man was now a crying and bleeding mess on the wooden floor. Shiro walked over to the man and opened a desk drawer. Tanaka grabbed the screaming man by his shirt and stuffed the man's head into the drawer. He tried to close the drawer, but the neck of the man was in the way. The man whose head was in the drawer desperately tried to pull himself out of his current situation. He tried to scream for help, but all that came out were the sounds of choking and strangling. The man's struggle eventually began to die down and finally it stopped.

Shiro opened the drawer and the new corpse slumped to the ground. Shiro closed the drawer and readjusted himself. Silence filled the room. After what felt like hours to the hired guns, Tanaka broke it with a demanding tone, "Now you see I will not hesitate to punish failure. Do not fail me again. Now leave." The employees couldn't wait to leave the room. They were so scared they ran. Two men burst through the doors and down the hallway as Cooper reached the doorway. As he saw the other men rush down the hall, two men holding pistols stepped in his way.

"Except for you, Cooper. I have a few more words for you."

Cooper stepped back into the room. "What is it," he asked with a grimace.

Tanaka leaned back in his chair. "Mr. Cooper, I realize that you don't particularly care about me or my operation, but I would like to let you know that we're kindred spirits."

"Yeah? How so?"

"We're both men who want to expand in our work. I came from Japan to oversee the taking of a new territory. You see, the expansion of my empire had grown stagnate. The other crime lords of my homeland feared my growing control and thought that I could eventually take over the entire

Yakuza and the country. They banded together to stop my power and sadly they succeeded. Whenever I tried to put more of my weapons or my drugs into a warehouse in their territory, it burned down. When I sent men to rob banks or intimidate weak government officials, the men were shot dead by my rivals. I couldn't move into their territory. They couldn't move into mine. It was a stalemate, but then your stupid government banned heroin. It was an opening. I could move in and corner the market here. I will monopolize on the desperate souls who will pay anything for the contents in my little vials of glass. Then I will take over the entire criminal underworld in this state."

"What does this have to do with me?"

As he said that a smile came across Tanaka's face. "Because I know why you took this job," he replied. "It's not because of the money. You haven't been able to expand. You've only been hired by locals for meaningless targets. Wife beaters, former employers, a man who knew too much, simple stuff. You wanted more. You wanted to be able to get some big employers. The bigger the employer the more connections they have. That's what I have, Cooper. I have connections to big people in Japan. Senators, mayors, crime lords, you name it I've got it. Soon I will be able to get more connections here in America. These could all be yours with a little letter of recommendation. All you have to do is cooperate with me smoothly on this one job and then you'll be promoted to one of the most hired hitmen in the business."

Cooper grinned, "That sounds very tempting."

"Do we have a deal, Cooper?"

"I think we do, Mr. Tanaka. I promise there won't be any more screwups."

"Good," Tanaka said as a ringing filled the room. Tanaka looked over to the phone rattling away next to him. "Would you excuse me, Mr. Cooper? I have an important phone call to take."

Cooper chuckled as he exited. "Sure thing. Maybe it's a dame that wants to be your new empress."

Tanaka allowed himself a small laugh. The laugh was partially from Cooper's joke. Most of it was from how he just played Cooper straight into his hand. "It's just too easy," he said aloud. Then he picked up the phone and brought it to his ear. "Hello, this is Tanaka."

After he uttered the phrase the sultry voice of a woman came onto the phone. "Hello Mr. Tanaka. I've heard that you have a party tonight, but me and my lover don't have an invitation."

"Oh? Why should I give you two invitations? This is a very exclusive party."

"Well my lover could work as security for your party. He's worked security at other parties. Maybe while he's away working, I could repay you in some way."

Shiro's eyes lit up from the proposition. He hadn't heard such an eager woman before especially in America. A few moments passed as he thought about the woman on the other end of the phone. He finally replied with his answer, "I think that will do. Where does your boyfriend work? I'll hire him to work security and I'll give you an invitation."

Ellen giggled on the other end of the line. *He's playing right into my hand,* she thought. The Nordic beauty opened her mouth again to let out her hypnotizing voice. "His name is Roger McKane and he owns his own security firm," she told him. "Don't tell him I asked you to hire him or that I will be there. I want to have a little alone time with you, Mr. Tanaka and don't worry he's not boyfriend. He's only one of my boy toys."

Tanaka was curious to meet this mysterious woman. Did she look as sexy as she sounded he wondered? "Oh, I won't. Where should I send your invitation?"

"You can send it to my hotel. Here's the address...."

After jotting it down, Tanaka said. "I can't wait to meet you in person, my dear.." Little did Mr. Tanaka know, he would regret those words by the end of the night.

The mansion was vast with its size and had several balconies to observe the guests below or look at the stars in the sky. It had an open courtyard inside the tall walls of its exterior like the English castles of yesteryear. Once one went through the courtyard, they could enter the mansion itself. It had long halls built with the finest mahogany wood in the state of California. It was a very nice mansion, but sadly the owner of it wasn't as nice as his property.

Ellen Patrick stepped out of her polished white vehicle. There were many eye-catching women at the party, but none compared to Ms. Patrick. She had an absolutely gorgeous red dress on, perfectly matching her black high heels. A white handbag hung unto her arm. She closed the door to the ivory vehicle and stepped onto the brick walkway that lead to the five-story mansion. She walked down the small scarlet brick road and entered through the gates of the courtyard. There she found a collection of about sixty men and women drinking champagne, wine, and snacking away at the various items that were on the snack table. There were some chairs and tables set out in the courtyard, but many guests weren't using them for various reasons. The doors of the mansion were open for guests to enter and admire the house, but the stairs were off limits due to Tanaka's "business" meetings.

Ellen grabbed a glass of champagne from a passing platter. She sipped away at the bubbly drink as she scanned the area for Tanaka's security forces. She found about twenty of them in various places of the mansion grounds until she was interrupted by a familiar voice.

"Ellen," Norman Johnson shouted to Ellen. He walked towards her with a glass of wine.

"Shit! Not now," she whispered through gritted teeth. She turned around and what she saw was surprising. Norman had shaved, brushed his hair, and by some miracle actually smelled nice. He had a new black tux with a new black tie to match instead of his old suit that was falling apart.

Her jaw dropped. "Wow. Norman you look great."

"Thank you, Ms. Patrick and don't worry I'm not here to hit on you. Just came over to say hi."

Well would you look at that, she thought. *He isn't trying to seduce me, he looks presentable, and he actually bathed. Apparently that little talk did work some much–needed magic.*

Ellen stopped herself from looking the new Norman Johnson over and spoke, "No offense, Norman, but you've changed a lot from the last time I saw you."

"None taken, Ms. Patrick. I had a bit of a life changing experience recently. It made me really look myself in the mirror and see how much of an asshole I was. Oh, I'm sorry for the language miss."

Ellen giggled, "It's fine, Norman."

"It was nice seeing you again. Now if you'll excuse me, I've got some other people to meet tonight."

Johnson walked away from Ellen towards the mayor, no doubt to apologize for past encounters with his wife. Ellen admired her handiwork from a distance with a smile. She was lost in thought from how much her warning as Domino Lady had worked. Suddenly a hand tapped her shoulder and a masculine voice spoke, "Hi Ellen"

Ellen jumped in fear. She barely made the landing to the ground with her black high heels. With a frustrated look drawn upon her face she turned to see who just scared her. The frustration disappeared immediately when she saw it was Roger McKane. She ran up to him and gave him a hug. "Hi

Roge," she said with the smile of a school girl. She closed her eyes as she buried her head into his firm, strong chest. After a few seconds passed, reality hit her eyes sprung open. She immediately pulled away. She stood two feet away from Roger and collected herself. She repeated her statement with a slight blush, "Hey Roge. What are you doing here?"

"Tanaka hired me to work security tonight."

"Oh, but what about your case?" she asked as if she was oblivious to the situation.

"Well," Roger looked around at the crowd of people around them and pulled in closer to Ellen. "Could we talk about that in a place more private?"

"Sure."

Roger guided Ellen over to a less crowded area and he continued in a hushed voice. "That's why I'm here. We have reason to believe that Shiro Tanaka caused the murders of those dock workers."

Ellen played like she was clueless. She could barely keep a smile from forming. She whispered, "Who's we and how'd you get that information?"

"I had help from a certain vigilante."

Ellen acted surprised. She whispered, "Oh that's so amazing, Roge. Was the Crimson Mask..or maybe the Black Bat? No, it couldn't have been him, he operates out of New York."

"It was the Domino Lady. Listen Ellen, its not safe here. The Domino Lady's coming, and I have no idea what's going to happen after she gets here."

"Aww you're worried about me."

Roger began to stumble on his words, "Yes. I mean, you're my friend of course I am. Look Ellen, this important. You need to leave."

"Okay, I'll go into the mansion and sneak out of a window. Then I'll go to my car."

"Be safe, Ellen."

"You too, Roge."

The blonde moved away from the detective and headed towards the open doors of the mansion. Her heels clicked on the stone stairs as she entered the modern castle. As she made her way through the guests in the hall she saw that the security guard was still at the stairway leading up to the second floor. Ellen knew exactly what to do.

The stair guard had been standing in the same spot ever since the party had begun. He was tired, weary, and of course bored. That all changed when a dame in a red dress caught his eye. He'd seen beautiful women before, but none of them compared to this one. Then the lady surprised him. She was coming closer and closer to him until they were inches apart.

"Hello, big guy," she said. The words of the angel delicately fell onto his ears like autumn leaves falling softly onto grass. The guard tried to respond, but he could not form any words. "Well aren't you going to say something, mister?"

"Uuuh umm of course, Miss," he replied. "I was just uuuuh…"

"Speechless?"

"Yes miss."

The woman in red gave him a seductive glare. "So you want to head up stairs?" she asked, her voice husky with desire.

The henchman looked around and shifted uncomfortably. He wanted to go, but he had a job to do. If Tanaka caught him, he'd kill him. "I don't know, miss. I've got a job to do."

The lady in red pouted. "But mister, I don't think anyone would mind," she reassured him. "You've been working so hard tonight. Don't you think you need a break?"

"Maybe."

The blonde tiptoed her fingers up the man's chest. "Come on, handsome. I'm feeling so lonely. Don't you want to give me some company?"

The woman's charms worked perfectly on the man. He couldn't resist her seductive grasp. With an idiotic grin, he agreed, "Yes miss. I think we can go upstairs."

The lady in red patted the man's head and give a cutesy reply, "Good boy. Now let's go."

The man led Ellen Patrick up the stairs. He walked down the second floor's hallway and stopped at a private bedroom. He opened the door to reveal a king-sized bed and various expensive trinkets. There were gorgeous paintings, delicately made furniture, and several emeralds. The man forgot about one of the room's fixtures though and he was quickly reintroduced to it when it collided with his head.

"What a moron," Ellen said with a bit of the broken vase in his head. She threw the remnants of the vase aside and stepped over the unconscious guard. "That was probably expensive. Tanaka certainly won't be happy."

She took off the red dress and let it fall to the floor. Normally when a woman takes off a dress it reveals a pair of bra and panties, but not Ellen. When Ellen takes off a gown, it normally reveals another dress. The black dress of the Domino Lady. She opened the hand bag and took out a piece of cloth that was folded into a square. The piece of fabric w.as quickly unfolded. It returned to its proper state as the cape of the Domino Lady.

Ellen swung the cape around to her back and tied the cape to her dress. The only costume piece left was her black domino mask. She pulled it out of her handbag and placed it onto the face of Ellen Patrick. To the naked eye, the woman known as Ellen Patrick disappeared from the room. The woman standing in her place was the crime–fighter known as the Domino Lady.

The Domino Lady reached into her handbag and pulled out a silver plated .22 caliber automatic pistol. With gun in hand, she stepped out of the room and entered the hallway. "Good," she whispered. "No one's around."

Domino Lady headed towards the staircase. She climbed the steps and then pressed her body onto a nearby wall. She carefully scanned the floor. The third floor only had two guards around and both were guarding the door that led to the stairs. There were several doors on the floor and one of them was very close to the staircase. Beside that door was a very large wardrobe. *Child's play,* she thought to herself. Domino Lady reached around the corner for the doorknob. She managed to grab it then she carefully turned the knob to not make a sound. After turning it fully, she pulled at the knob. The door cracked open, but from her position she couldn't open it all the way. She placed her hand within the door crack then with all her might, flung the door open. She quickly withdrew her arm back to her hiding place.

The door opening had the intended effect on the guards. The duo rushed to the opened door. "Who's there," one of them cried out.

When they arrived, the guards entered the room to find the intruder. This was a mistake on their part. Domino Lady had rushed to the door and had quietly shut them in. As the two were looking around she pushed the wardrobe in front of the door. When the guards realized that the intruder was not inside the room but in the hallway, it was already too late. The wardrobe completely blocked the door and there was no other way out. Domino Lady made her way down the hallway as the two guards desperately tried to wedge the door open.

The masked avenger opened the doors to the stairs and resumed her journey. She approached the fourth level of the mansion with caution. *It's probably harder from here on,* she thought. She reached the top step and to no one's surprise, it was. There was a man with a tommy gun and three men with katanas guarding the staircase. *Really? Swords! Who uses swords in this century?*

Domino Lady scanned the area for some kind of distraction. There were no nearby doors that she could lead the men into and no way she could lead them away. She had to fight them. *Great,* she thought. *Maybe I won't die.*

From her hiding space, she aimed her gun at the man with the machine gun. She didn't want to kill him, but she didn't want him to kill her either. She took a deep breath and whispered, "Let's get this over with." She reluctantly pulled the trigger. The bullet caught the guard in the arm. The man screamed as the blood from the wound poured out and changed his tuxedo from a black color to a dark red. Seeing their companion wounded, the katana wielding guards ran at the Domino Lady.

Domino Lady aimed at them, but she couldn't find a decent shot. If she fired, she'd either miss or kill one of them. Neither was an option and so she did the only thing she could do. She ran down the hallway towards them. The all collided in the middle of the hallway. Domino Lady ducked as one of the katanas swung towards her head. Then she dove as one of the swords sliced through the air towards her vertically.

She landed onto the floor but had no time to relax. Another sword was coming down. It was too close to dodge and too fast to give her time to think. By instinct, Domino Lady held her pistol tight with both hands and tried to block the deadly blade. Her left hand was on top of the gun barrel and her right was clutching the handle. She closed her eyes and hoped that this wasn't the end.

Instead of feeling pain, she heard a loud clang. She opened her eyes and a wave of relief hit her. The blade had stopped directly next to the trigger guard of her gun. *I'm not dead,* she thought. *But how do I get out of this one?*

"Hold her still," one of the swordsmen yelled. Domino Lady looked up to see the other guard rushing at her.

Oh my God! He's going to chop my head off, she thought. *I've got to find a way out of this quick.*

She looked back at the present danger and saw the hate in his eyes. A billion ideas of escape rushed through her head in that moment, but there was only one that she decided on. She looked directly into his eyes and asked him, "Hey, do you want a kiss?"

The man's hate turned into confusion. The pressure of the katana softened as the gears in his head turned. "What?"

In an instant, The Domino Lady turned her gun and rolled out of the way from the katana. Once the weapon's blade was embedded into the wooden floor, she aimed at the man's legs and fired her gun three times.

"Hold her still."

Each bullet entered the attacker. The man fell over and yelled in pain. "Maybe the nurse will give you one," she suggested.

The approaching swordsman's was almost upon her. Before he could strike, the Domino Lady fired another round right into his shoulder. The small hole in his shoulder caused the man's knees to buckle. He fell to the floor with little grace. Ellen picked herself up using the hall's nearest hall's wall as a crutch.

Suddenly a knife struck inches away from her face. The wielder of the deadly dagger was disappointed in the missing of his target. The clean silver blade was now buried in the wall. Without hesitation Ellen aimed her pistol at the blade and fired.

The blade disappeared and was replaced with hundreds of metal shards. They shimmered in the air for a second then fell to the ground like raindrops. The Domino Lady's brown eyes were filled with rage. Her hand held the barrel of her .22 caliber in an iron grip. The vigilante swung her gun into the man's head with a great wrath. The makeshift club hit its target and the guard quickly fell unconscious.

The Nordic beauty looked around at the fallen guards. The fight wasn't exactly something she wanted to do, but she couldn't deny that she really enjoyed doing it. The thrill and danger of being The Domino Lady was a rush to her. She could never deny it. Sometimes it could be scary, but the ride was well worth all the bumps in the road.

After readjusting herself, Ellen stepped over the bodies and began her journey up to the next floor. Little did she know there was a commotion outside.

The Domino Lady's gun shots had been heard throughout the mansion. Unfortunately, Tanaka's men also heard the shots. The twenty outside guards entered the mansion with guns at the ready. Roger McKane stormed the house with them. He didn't have the same objective as the other hired guns. He knew who fired those gunshots. He knew that The Domino Lady had arrived.

The squad of men entered the second floor. While the other guards were checking rooms, he moved up to the door closest to the staircase. Roger opened the door only to find an unconscious man and a smashed vase. Roger quickly closed the door. The last thing he needed was more guards. After closing the door, what seemed to be the head guard approached him.

"Did you find anything," the man asked.

"No," Roger lied.

"Okay," the fellow turned around and yelled down the hall. "We move onto the next floor, men!"

The group closed the doors and stepped up to the next floor. Roger followed closely behind them. When the men arrived, they found a wardrobe in front of a door. Behind the wooden blockade, two men pushed against their wooden prison.

The chief signaled his men, "You three push that out of the way. The rest of you check the other doors!"

Roger McKane headed down the hallway to the last door. As soon as he reached it, he bolted through the doors to the stairway. Luckily, the guards hadn't noticed Roger's recent departurel, but he had to act fast. The private eye rushed up the stairway to find something to block the door.

When Roger reached the top step, he was surprised by the sight that lay before him. Four unconscious men with weapons lying about the delicate wooden floor. The Domino Lady certainly had cleaned house. Roger didn't have time to worry about the unconscious men right then. There was still a door to block.

Roger looked through the first room and found a wardrobe. "The irony," he muttered. Roger pushed the wardrobe out of the room. Time was not on his side. He was almost to the stairs when he heard the voice of the guard boss.

"Clear! We're moving up." Roger's eyes widened in panic. With all his strength he pushed the wardrobe to the staircase. He set himself to push the heavy object down, but he heard the door creak. *The door,* he thought. The thought rang through his head like a siren.

Roger jumped down the stairs and slammed the door. Roger pushed against the door. He was practically glued to it. A voice cried out from the other side, "Holy shit! He almost got my hand!"

The lead guard ignored his man's reaction. His main concern was finding and killing the intruder. He stepped forward with a grimace on his face. "I hate delays," he muttered. He drew out his gun from its holster held it at the ready. "Listen up, intruder," he yelled out. "I'm giving you three seconds to open that door or else I will break it down and drag you out myself. One, two, th—"

Roger yelled out from the other side of the door, his body still pressed against it, "Okay, I'm going to open the door. Just give me a few seconds." He desperately needed away out he'd walked into.

The head guard smirked. He yelled back to Roger, "Okay, son. We don't want to hurt you. We just want to escort you off the property." Then he whispered to his men, "Aim at the door. If he doesn't come out in five seconds, fire."

Roger's panicked mind raced through about twenty ideas. He thought none of them were good except for one. A smile formed on his face as he drew his gun and aimed. "Okay, I'm coming out."

Suddenly there was the sound of a gun shot and then a bump on the door. The guards looked at each other in confusion. "D—did did he just kill himself?"

Another guard replied. "I mean, maybe. Why else would he fire a gun?"

The boss growled. "Open the door, you idiots."

The closest one to the doors tried to push it open. It didn't budge. He tried again. Nothing "I can't, sir"

More bumps on the door echoed through the hall. The guard's face distorted with anger. "Damn it. He's still alive."

After having escaped through the back hallway, Roger once again charged up the flight of stairs to the second landing. There he began anything he could and throwing it down the stairs with the wardrobe. The wardrobe was now missing one of its legs. Roger's bullet had shattered it. Then the wardrobe tumbled down the stairs with ease after that. Roger emptied the room with incredible speed. Various chairs, tables, and other furniture were added to the pile in front of the door.

After emptying the room, he dragged the unconscious bodies and pushed a cabinet in front of it. He didn't need any more company. While he was there he found several boxes filled with heroin bottles. He took several bottles for evidence to show the police. After he left the room with several bottles in his pocket, he took up the machine gun lying on the floor and called the police from one of the room's phones. With the police on their way, he opened the doors to the next floor and headed up to meet up with the Domino Lady.

He didn't know what to expect, but he knew for certain that the two of them were ending Tanaka's plans tonight.

The Domino Lady hurried up the stairwell to the final floor. With pistol in hand, she passed the final step and burst through the hallway doors. It was empty. It was silent. Ellen began walking down the hallway. *Tanaka*

must have expected me to die before I got up here. Sorry to disappoint.

Ellen finally reached the door. Her delicate hand grabbed the door knob and twisted it. She pushed it open and a creak rang out through the dark room. The only light was from the only light sources came from the moon, the open door and Shiro's desk lamp. Domino Lady's silver pistol shimmered in the moonlight as it pointed its deadly stare at the crime lord. Shiro barely noticed the Valkyrie at his doorway. He was too busy with the paperwork that lay before him. His eyes didn't waver from his pen and paper.

"Put your hands up, stand, and face the wall," Ellen said with nothing but bitterness for the man.

Shiro paused and put down his pen. He looked up from his paperwork and smiled. He leaned back in his chair and faced the woman before him. "So you must be the fabled Domino Lady," he said coldly. "I've heard much about you."

"Get up."

"I'm guessing you were the woman on the phone then. Shame. It could have been a nicer evening, but you will do."

"Shut up and get out of that chair."

"I will, but I'd like to thank you first."

"Thank me?"

"Why of course. Without you none of this would be possible." Domino Lady walked closer to Tanaka's desk. "What do you mean? You kill people. You smuggle drugs. I never helped you with that. I never would help you with any of your crimes."

"Oh, but you have. You see, all your crime fighting has been wonderful for my business. You've taken down so many crime lords here in your state of California. There isn't any competition. No one is a threat to me here. You made California a land ripe for conquest. Think of it as the Spanish Conquistadors and the Aztec Empire. There was no competition back then and there is no competition now. It will be a slaughter."

"You're a monster."

"Maybe. Cooper, you may proceed."

A figure suddenly charged out of the darkness and slammed her into the nearest wall. In the sudden attack her weapon fell to the floor. She didn't need to ask who Cooper was, she had a definitive answer. The tall, bald man had her throat in his hands and her body pressed against the wall. The Domino Lady tried to tear the force away from her throat but without success. She tried to kick the man off of her, but alas it failed as well. Ellen struggled to breathe, and the sounds of her choking echoed throughout the room. *Is this the end?*, she thought. *No, it will not end here.*

Ellen reached for anything to hit her attacker with, but nothing was in reached. Her hand grazed pass her side and she felt a familiar cylinder on her side. Ellen's eyes lit up.

She quickly reached to her garter belt and pulled out the syringe filled with the knockout drug. She raised the needle above her hand and then shoved it into her foe. The needle stabbed into Cooper's shoulder and Ellen quickly pressed down upon the plunger. The drug flowed through the veins of the hitman. With seconds he slumped to the floor.

Ellen gasped for air and steadied herself. She would indeed live to fight another night. Tanaka was surprised by Cooper's easy defeat. He opened one of the drawers to his desk and pulled out a pistol. "No matter," he said. "Cooper was a weak American just like you."

"I wouldn't say that," a male voice said. Light filled the room as Roger Mckane flicked on the wall. "The only weakling, I see here isn't an American."

Domino Lady was delighted to see her ally. "Roge."

Roger smiled. "Hey Domino, glad to see you too."

Ellen's red lips formed into a smile. "It took you long enough."

"Well at least I showed up. By the way, I called the police. He's not going anywhere."

"They won't believe you," Tanaka interrupted. "You're just hired security."

"Detective actually," Roger responded. "I've worked very closely with them over the years and since we've got you're assassin at the docks right here. Also the harbormaster told us that the shipment of all those crates was yours. Connect the dots and its going to be real hard to squirm out of the judge's sentence. What do you think it'll be, Domino? Life sentence or death sentence?"

The masked blonde playfully brought her finger to the tip of her chin. "I don't know, McKane. Maybe he'll decide by flipping a coin."

Tanaka pointed his gun at the duo. He screamed "You son of a—"

Tanaka was interrupted by a pain in his shoulder. He looked down at the growing red splotch on his tuxedo. He then moved his eyes to the smoking barrel held by the lady in the black dress and white cape. "Don't insult my partner, Tanaka. And don't ever try to shoot him."

The Domino Lady reached down to Cooper's unconscious body and pulled out the syringe. "It's a shame I had to waste this on him. Now I don't know how we're going to knock him out before the cops get here."

Roger pulled out a glass vial from his jacket pocket. "We could use this," he responded with a mischievous grin. "Would be a very poetic end to Tanaka."

Tanaka grabbed his arm in pain. "You wouldn't dare," he said coldly.

The Domino Lady grabbed the vial and inserted the needle into the white liquid. She pulled the plunger and the heroin filled the syringe's glass container. "Afraid to get high on your own supply, Tanaka?"

Roger moved over to the desk as Domino Lady threw the empty vial onto the desk. Shiro Tanaka desperately tried to raise his pistol to shoot them, but the pain in his arm was too much. Roger grabbed Tanaka's gun and tossed it aside. He held Tanaka down as the femme fatale approached. Tanaka struggled against McKane's hold. "Stop it, you stupid bitch," Shiro screamed.

Ellen slapped the crime lord's face hard. "This is for those dock workers. This for everyone you have or could have hurt." She stabbed the needle through his arm and pressed down on the plunger. The heroin entered the once powerful man's body and quickly began to take effect. He skin began to sweat, he felt like he was going to throw up, and finally he began to sleep.

Roger let go of the criminal and The Domino Lady laid down her syringe. "No point in using this now. It's contaminated with that garbage."

Roger walked around from behind the desk. "Thanks for saving me again. That's the second time this week I almost got shot."

"Oh, you big baby," she chuckled. "I get almost shot more than that every night."

The two laughed together for a minute. "I guess this is the end for our partnership," Roger sighed. "The case has been solved, Tanaka's plans are ruined, and we have enough evidence to put him in the chair or in a cell for decades."

"Yeah. It's been great working with you, McKane. Maybe we can do this again some other time."

"Hopefully."

The sirens of police cars and the screech of rubber tires filled the air as the two stood silently. The police stepped out of their cars, rushed past the tables in the courtyard and stepped into the mansion. Roger finally spoke to the vigilante, "I guess I better go help them round up the criminals. Do you have a way out?"

"Of course, I do."

"Well goodbye, Domino," Roger said as he began to walk out the door.

"It's been a pleasure."

"Wait." The Domino Lady rushed over to him. She grabbed his head and kissed his lips. The kiss lasted for what felt like an eternity. A perfect eternity. The duo's lips finally parted from each other. Although they didn't want to they had to. "I'm going to miss you, McKane. Would you do me a favor?"

"Of course."

Domino Lady gave the private eye a smile, "Give that kiss to someone special. Like that Patrick girl."

Roger stumbled back a bit as he heard the masked woman's request. "Uuuh, heh—I don't know, Domino. That's, mmm, quite a favor. I mean do you think, she'd want me to? Do you have any other favor in mind or uhhh is tha—?"

The vigilante cut him off, "Roger, this is the only favor I have in mind. Remember I've saved your life twice in the past two days."

"True, but—"

"No buts. Ellen Patrick's going to love that, I promise."

"O-okay. I guess I do owe you one. Actually two."

"Yes, you do. Now go off and help your boys in blue. Then meet Ellen and give her a kiss for me."

"All right, Domino," Roger said as he headed out the door. "I'll see you later."

Roger ran down the hallway and down the stairs. Domino Lady grinned knowingly. "You certainly will."

Domino Lady hurried back to Tanaka's office and rummaged through the office. She finally found what she was looking for. A roll of tape. She tore off a piece and hurried to the door. She closed the door and reached into her garter belt. She pulled out a black card engraved with white lettering. She placed the tape on the card then placed it onto the door. "Thank God, I didn't forget," she said to herself.

Then she melted into the night. The police would get her message from the black card awaiting them. On the card was written five simple words. Compliments of the Domino Lady.

The End

WHERE WERE THE DAMES

*W*hen one considers all the hundreds of great pulp characters created before, during, and after the Great Depression, the miniscule number of female characters boggles the mind. Apparently the pre–World War II image of dames was the object to be rescued by the macho male hero. Yet, there were exceptions in the women who fought alongside the Shadow, the Spider, and others. All of them equal to their respective tasks. But as for those lucky enough to be the primary star of their own series, Domino Lady stands out and the most recognizable. Ellen Patrick is a joy to write, to get to know and to watch as she goes into action. We hope you will agree. This was fun.

KELLY NOLAN – Is a professional journalist with a flair for action adventure fiction. He loves all things pulp. This is his first work for Airship 27 Production.

BLUE SAPPHIRES AND PLATINUM BLONDES

by Kevin Findley

April 15, 1938

*M*oments like this were what thrilled the masked blonde the most. Looking at the driver's mirror, she could see the prowl car behind her with its light flashing and hear its siren wailing. For just a moment, the young woman felt every care lift off of her before the police officer started to close the gap.

She downshifted at the last possible second and took the turn on the inside lane, risking a head-on collision. The prowl car's driver shifted too late and skidded along both lanes. He crumpled the right, rear fender on the guardrail, but continued after her.

The masked beauty looked back again and then laughed with glee and relief. She had missed the on-coming auto at the end of her turn by less than a foot, threw gravel everywhere, but kept the stolen roadster mostly on the road and moving forward. The rest of Palos Verde Drive to South Western was fairly straight, so she opened it up and put more distance between herself and her pursuer.

As the car leaped forward, she ran her thumb across the large, sapphire ring on her left hand for a moment. It was the sparkling, blue icing on her purloined cake. Stealing from criminals and the crooked politicians who covered for them was starting to become routine, so being interrupted made for a much more exciting evening. She was quickly shaken out of her reverie though when she saw the prowl car catching up again; its larger engine overtaking the roadster that only looked fast.

Next time I check under the hood before I steal a car. Then she looked ahead, laughed and thought, *I guess I'll just have to outsmart him.*

With a grin and a fresh thrill up her spine, she swerved the stolen car over far enough to kick up a cloud of dust. She stayed in the on-coming lane to obscure the view for the cop and watched in the rear-view mirror as the prowler nearly stood on its nose and still failed to miss the stalled auto only half pulled over to the shoulder. The daring young woman threw the roadster in reverse to check on the driver and leave a message.

As Patrolman Ralph Harris' eyes began to clear, the first thing he saw was the card tucked into the driver's window. Printed in white on the black cardstock were the words, 'Compliments of the Domino Lady'!

The excitement started when the wife of crooked Councilman Reuben Victor returned home early. The Domino Lady had just finished searching Victor's office and went upstairs. There was no safe to match the key she found hidden in a false book, so the bedroom was the next likely place.

As she opened the safe and removed the top tray, her delicately shaped ears heard the front door open.

"Grab a bottle of champagne and meet me upstairs Ralph. Reuben is going to be too busy at Granville Delacroix's card game to be home until one or two in morning and I need someone to scrub my back."

"I'll be there before you can pour in the bubble bath Agnes!"

As Mrs. Victor kicked off her shoes and unzipped her dress, she looked over to see the Domino Lady standing in front of her closet. She sneered at the young woman.

"Wrong night honey. Reuben's still at the party. If you hurry, you can meet him there to play cops and robbers." She jerked her thumb toward the open doorway. "Now get out of here you little tramp before I have Ralph down there beat you with a sap."

"I'm a thief, not a tramp."

"I'll crack you one in the mouth myself you little …!" Agnes' mouth closed tight when she finally saw the open safe. She looked back at the younger woman as the Domino Lady waved her left hand with Agnes' sapphire ring on her index finger.

"Believe me now?"

Agnes looked scared for the first time. "Give me that!" Then she charged the younger woman, grabbing for her hand and cursing like a sailor. The Domino Lady punched her with a right-handed gammen-tsuki over the sternum. As Agnes went to her knees gasping, the masked bombshell quickly injected her with the second half of a knockout drug to keep her quiet. The first half went to the maid unconscious in Councilman Victor's office.

After making certain the high society fishwife was breathing normally, the Domino Lady grabbed the last jewelry tray from the still open safe, and a large stack of cash. She dropped everything into a velvet bag she also took from the safe, and quickly exited the bedroom.

As the Domino Lady moved to the stairs, she could just see over the rail that Ralph was walking across the foyer with a bottle of wine and two glasses. His hat was pushed back on his head and formal jacket unbuttoned at the collar.

Well, she thought. *He is a big, handsome lug. Kind of like Li'l Abner.*

"Agnes! Your husband put the champagne under lock and key. I hope red is okay. It's, uh, Bo-jou-lay?"

The Domino Lady pulled quickly back just in time to keep the officer from seeing her as he looked up.

"Agnes?" *She's probably in the shower already.* Patrolman Harris got halfway up the stairs and realized he forgot the corkscrew. He spun on his heel and went back to the kitchen. Ralph never heard the lithe, young woman move down the stairs behind him.

As Harris found the corkscrew, he felt a small hand push him off-balance. He grinned and started to push back just as stars filled his eyes and then everything went black.

"Oh no!" She looked at the broken bottle in her hand and then over to the wine rack. "The '34 was a poorer year than this '32. I should have hit him with that!"

The Domino Lady moved quickly out of the Victor house to the car she parked next door. Knocking a man on the head was not as exact as inserting a syringe in his neck, but there was nothing left after dosing Mrs. Victor. As she climbed into the roadster, she looked back to see Harris stumble through the front door.

He grabbed at an empty holster and then looked up to see the masked woman smile and toss his revolver into the fountain bubbling in the front yard. Snarling, Harris jumped into the patrol car, hit the starter and drove after her.

Ellen Patrick smiled at the memory from two days ago as she leaned over another rail and looked out across her view of Long Beach. In the distance a bit, she could see the Navy Yard and a few of the larger ships docked there. The number had increased over the last eight months since Japan had clashed with the Chinese Army in Peiping and then destroyed the U.S. gunship *Panay* less than two weeks before Christmas. The April wind blowing across the deck of her friend's apartment made her shiver from more than just the cold.

"Ellen! Come in before you catch your death!"

The vivacious blonde looked down at the tailored pantsuit she wore with matching jacket and then turned her head to see Anna standing inside the sliding door, tapping one foot impatiently.

"I did not invite you here to watch you moon over a bunch of sailors that aren't even close enough to see you wave at them."

"All right Anna, I'll come in."

Anna Daniels had been a classmate at Berkeley. Until Ellen arrived, she was the top girl in their social level. Anna had hair so black that it glowed in moonlight with eyes almost as dark. Despite her stunning beauty, Ellen outshone Anna. There were many blonde-haired, brown-eyed beauties in California, but Ellen Patrick had that quality which could not only stop traffic, the drivers got out of their automobiles and offered her the keys.

At first there was an intense dislike, but when Anna learned that Ellen had lost her mother at an early age like Anna had when she was ten, they bonded closely. Each one was now the other's biggest cheering section. When Ellen received word in Japan that her Father had been killed, Anna was waiting for her when her ship docked.

"I remember you catching a cold every fall and winter at Berkeley, Ellen. I'd have thought you'd know better by now."

Ellen smiled as she remembered how Anna would fuss over her when she had so much as the sniffles. *Her pupils are in good hands,* she thought. The raven-haired girl had accepted a teaching position at Sterling Academy after graduation.

"I suppose I'll have to get Marion to play mother hen a little better and keep me indoors."

Anna rolled her eyes. "Oh don't be silly Ellen, you couldn't pay your poor housekeeper enough for that additional duty. Now go clean up a bit, Michael will be here soon. "

What was supposed to be a temporary job while she 'caught' a husband, turned into a love of teaching that surprised even Anna. Fortunately, the fiancée she had recently netted was also an instructor at Sterling and Michael Garner laughed to think of themselves one day as a pair of little, old teachers grading papers together and mixing up their reading glasses.

What would she think, Ellen wondered as she re-entered the home, *at some of the risks I take now?*

For nearly two years, the young socialite had led, and even enjoyed her double life as a thorn in the side of the local underworld and the police. As the Domino Lady, Ellen was slowly sending to jail everyone that she could prove to herself had been involved in her father's death. A few of them underestimated the masked avenger's resolve and now were facing their eternal punishment.

Despite her successes, Ellen knew the people who had ordered Owen Patrick's death were still out there. She hoped she had hurt them, but knew they would not feel the impact of their actions until they were in prison.

Dad believed in the system, devoted and gave his life to it. I have to try and make them stand up in a courtroom to face what they've done. Even if it isn't directly for his death.

Ellen finished washing up and went back into Anna's compact dining room.

"Have you had another break-in since last year?"

"No, the police never caught the thief, but at least they got my jewelry back from a pawnshop. That Detective Taylor was very nice about everything."

"I'm sure he was dear." Ellen used Anna's break-in as an excuse to meet Steven Taylor of the Long Beach Police. He had unknowingly provided vital information that helped the Domino Lady break up a warehouse theft ring.

I should probably show up at his office for lunch soon, just to catch up. Ellen thought. Then she noticed Anna putting down a fourth place setting.

"I thought this was a social gathering Anna."

"It's more social with an even number Ellen. This way you'll have someone to talk to when Michael and I are staring into each other's eyes."

Like most engaged and recently married women, Anna was convinced all of her single friends should be just as happy. So far, she had set Ellen up with two of her fellow teachers and one of Michael's cousins. Each of them were pleasant young men, but Ellen had no desire to consider marriage until she had put the last conspirator in her Father's death behind bars.

"If you start planning any wedding except your own Anna dear, I'll jump the rail on your deck and run off down the beach."

A knock at the door stopped Anna's reply. She ran to the door and threw it open before Ellen could issue any more threats.

"Michael! Come in darling and bring your friend with you." Ellen watched the two embrace and then looked behind them for Michael's friend. He was slightly shorter than Michael's six-foot frame, probably 5'10", which made him 5 inches taller than Ellen.

"Ellen, may I introduce Carl Echols? He's the new athletic director for Sterling Academy."

Carl nodded at Ellen and stepped forward. His sandy blonde hair had just been clipped into a fresh crew cut which set off his blue eyes. He was as trim as Michael, but Carl was a little broader in the shoulders.

"It's a pleasure meeting you Ellen."

Well, Ellen thought, *at least he's pretty to look at over dinner.* She took Carl's hand.

"We'll see about that."

Carl Echols turned out to be an excellent conversationalist. He knew the right topics and the right people through his students at Sterling. Even with all that, he did not bore Ellen silly as the rest of her previous dinner companions had done.

"Carl also played tennis at UCLA Ellen."

"OK Anna! He is an all-round athlete with a good job and secure future." She turned to look at Carl. "Tell me your real, last name is Getty and Anna can have us married by tomorrow morning."

"Ellen!" As Anna tried to look appalled, Michael laughed, and Carl had the decency to look embarrassed at it all.

Anna got up from the table and pointed Ellen to the kitchen.

"We're serving dessert before you say something else to ruin an otherwise lovely evening. Now mush Ellen!"

With both men now laughing at her, Ellen started into the kitchen with all the dignity she could muster. When she saw Anna still pointing like she was one of her students, Ellen put on a pout and placed her left hand on her hip. Then she added an extra sway to her walk that stopped the laughter as quick as it started. As she walked past Anna, Ellen said in her best Mae West impression:

"Careful what you wish for Sister."

The laughter started again and continued through dessert.

Gregor Minsky was not the Domino Lady's usual fence. Max Finnegan recommended two weeks earlier that she take any purloined gems there since he was going to visit family in Ireland for a month. At least that was what he told the Domino Lady before leaving just ahead of an arrest warrant. Max also charged only a nominal referral fee since he liked the young woman and how she irritated the cops.

The blonde avenger handed over the other jewels first, keeping back only the ring along with the matching earrings and brooch she discovered after returning home. After thirty minutes of examination and haggling, the Domino Lady felt she had a good price.

"I do have something else for you to look over." As she handed over the ring, Gregor gasped loudly and stared at it for a long moment. Instead of examining it under a jeweler's loupe though, he pulled out a stack of movie magazines from under the counter and began flipping through them. After a minute of this, the Domino Lady interrupted.

"Well, what do you think? I know the ring is a little gaudy, but I have the …"

"It's exquisite!" Gregor interrupted with a look of horror. "How can you say that about the poor woman's ring?"

"Poor woman?"

"Well yes, the …" The fence looked up in surprise and turned the magazine he opened around for the Domino Lady to see. "You didn't know this belonged to Jean Harlow?"

Ten minutes later, the Domino Lady knew the details of Harlow's last days, her death, and how the missing ring was slowly becoming a Hollywood legend.

"So we really don't know what happened to it?" She asked.

"No. There are conflicting stories if she was wearing it when she went to the hospital or if it was left in her dressing room when they loaded her in the ambulance. William Powell gave it to her as a Christmas present in 1936."

"That's right! The gossip columns called it the ugliest engagement ring ever all through Valentine's Day."

Gregor sadly nodded. "That was very hurtful to Jean. Powell made it clear it wasn't an engagement ring, but the gossip columnists just wouldn't leave it alone."

"So the real mystery is what happened to it."

"Yes, Mama Jean Harlow let Powell look over their home and the studio claimed that they sealed Jean's dressing room suite immediately after they took her to the hospital. Everyone just assumed that the other had the ring and didn't even ask about it until after she died."

Gregor hesitated for a moment, but pushed ahead. "I have to ask Miss Domino, where did you 'find it'?"

"Don't worry about the ring." She scooped it up from the counter, dropped it back into the bag with the earrings and brooch, and turned to leave. "I'm keeping it safe for now!"

After listening to Gregor tell the tale, the Domino Lady decided to return the ring to William Powell before she even drove halfway home. She also realized that she couldn't just sneak it back into Powell's home or mail it to him. The young woman needed to hear more about Jean first.

She pulled off to the side of the road, placed the car in neutral and set the hand brake. The Domino Lady looked around quickly, and then removed her mask. Ellen Patrick covered her blond curls with a driving cap and shrugged on a short jacket over the white evening dress. A moment later, she put the roadster back into gear and drove home.

Marion was long gone by the time the former debutante walked into her home, but had left two messages for Ellen. One was a request to meet from a colleague of her late father. A former Assistant District Attorney, Edwin Tapper was a little dull, but pleasant, and Ellen could not think of an excuse to avoid him. He had called her several times since Owen Patrick's murder to update her before he left for private practice, but since then, no one called her from the DA's office, and Edwin had only called her once in the last six months.

The second message was from Anna. Carl Echols had enjoyed his evening, and wanted to know if Ellen would like to join him this Thursday for tennis and then a late lunch. It was Spring Break for Sterling Academy, and he wanted to take advantage of it. As a Sterling faculty member, Carl had limited memberships at several of the area country clubs.

"Well why not," Ellen said to herself. "I haven't played in almost a month."

On Tuesday morning, Ellen called and made plans with both men. Edwin Tapper was available on Wednesday, so Ellen let Marion know they would have a guest for lunch that day. She then raced to the nearest news-stand, grabbed the local papers and glossy magazines, trying to make certain when Powell would be home. The radium treatments the actor was undergoing for cancer was apparently working just as the doctors had promised and he hoped very soon to begin his next movie. Powell was recuperating from the last treatment in the mountains, but was to return home on Friday.

She spent the early afternoon at the library, going through back issues of Silver Screen, Photoplay, Look, and the newspapers, trying to find out more about Harlow, Powell, and their relationship. Despite the attempt of many writers to make it look like a young actress hitching her wagon to Powell's star, there was obviously a genuine affection between the two.

Perhaps they were just mad Powell and Myrna Loy weren't married in real life like in the movies. Eventually, Ellen found one of the obituaries for Jean in the June 7th late edition.

Rising starlet, Jean Harlow, passed away today at the age of 26. Her death, according to her doctors, was due to recently diagnosed uremic poisoning.

Born in Kansas City, Missouri, Jean's mother brought her to Los Angeles in 1921 to pursue the Hollywood dream. Jean married Charles McGrew in 1927, but the pressures of pursuing an acting career ended the marriage in 1929. She was spotted by Hal Roach while working as an extra and he quickly signed her to a contract and put her in the Laurel and Hardy comedy, Double Whoopee.

Jean's 'big break' came when Howard Hughes cast her in Hell's Angels the following year. She continued in further films like The Secret Six and Platinum Blonde. In 1932, MGM bought out her contract from Hughes and quickly cast her in Red-Headed Woman. Anita Loos wrote the part of Lil Andrews specifically for Jean to showcase her natural, comedic talent. MGM followed-up that smash appearance with a string of movies with Clark Gable like Red Dust and Bombshell.

As her professional life and fame grew, personal happiness eluded Jean. Her second husband, MGM executive Paul Bern, died in 1932 after only three months of marriage. In 1933, Jean married Harold Rosson, but she and the cinematographer divorced the following year.

Love bloomed a final time for Jean when she met William Powell on the set of Reckless. While off and on at the beginning, the two were inseparable from 1936 until her death this morning. Powell was at her bedside, along with Jean's mother, cousin, and stepfather.

The next morning, Ellen woke early to help Marion prepare lunch and opened the door to greet Edwin personally.

"You're just in time for lunch Edwin! Please come to the dining room so we can talk until Marion brings in the meal."

"Thank you for seeing me Ellen." He gestured around him. "Especially here at home. It brings back some excellent memories of Owen."

"You're welcome Edwin. I never get to see any of Father's friends now. I'd almost think none of you were really interested in me, and were only humoring me because I'm Owen Patrick's daughter."

"I'm sure that's not true."

"Oh, so you do have a personal interest?" Ellen smiled just a little brighter and leaned forward. Edwin leaned back a little embarrassed, but cleared his throat and continued.

"Well, I suppose this visit is related to Owen to be honest. I have a question about any notes or other papers that you might have found since his death."

"Murder you mean." Ellen's voice hardened enough for Edwin to notice.

"I'm sorry, Ellen. I didn't mean to offend you. Even after seven years with the DA's office, it's still a difficult word when talking about a friend."

"That's all right Edwin." Ellen abashedly leaned back. "What exactly are you looking for?"

"I was asked a question about work Owen and I did on a case three-and-a-half years ago. There was a note that he and I were interviewing a witness together with his lawyer in Seal Beach, but his lawyer noted that I was the only one there."

"Is it that important?" Ellen asked.

"Probably not. Other cases come up, and either of us might have to go interview someone else or meet an informant." He shrugged. "It's not uncommon, but the bureaucrat involved is like a dog with an old bone. There's no longer any meat, but he just won't let go of it."

"I'm sorry Edwin, but an investigator with the DA's office came and took everything work related from the house. There was nothing left." *Until I found Dad's coded datebook.*

The datebook had helped Ellen on more than one case, and she wished now she had looked through her father's papers more carefully before turning them over. Especially since she suspected someone in the DA's office was part of the group that killed him.

"I thought that was the situation."

"Why didn't anyone from Dad's old office contact me?"

"That's all right Edwin. What exactly are you looking for?"

"I asked the same question. The person I spoke to was very dismissive; he felt that you wouldn't know anything useful and if you had found something, you probably wouldn't understand it and threw it out. He believed I might be able to coax something useful out of you." Edwin paused a moment.

"However, I understand you're Owen's daughter and what that means. Your degree isn't from a law school and you may not understand all the legal terminology, but you wouldn't have thrown anything in the trash if you thought it made the difference in an innocent man staying in jail or a guilty one going free."

"Thank you Edwin."

"You're welcome. To be honest, after the phone call, this was a good excuse for me to see you and catch up. I'm sorry I haven't called before now."

"That's all right, beginning private practice after so many years with the D.A. must take up a lot of time."

"Well that ..." Edwin hesitated for a moment. "... and getting engaged."

"What?! Why didn't you start with that? Congratulations!" She looked up as Marion came in with their lunch.

"Did you hear that Marion? Edwin is engaged."

"I did, Miss Patrick. Congratulations Mr. Tapper."

"Thank you Marion." The housekeeper finished laying out lunch and then departed. Edwin turned back to Ellen. "Her name is Natalie Brooks."

"How did you meet?"

Between bites, Edwin told her how they had met on a blind date set up by a senior partner in his new law firm. She was an acquaintance of the partner's wife and, after five years, had just given up trying to make a living as an actress.

"Young girl giving up her dreams of stardom?" Ellen teased.

"Actually no, she was doing well as a character actress, but in the last year she had only one speaking part and three crowd scenes after going to dozens of auditions. She believes that she simply isn't on the preferred list for several new casting directors." Edwin shook his head in disbelief.

"I don't see it. She's only ten years younger than I am, but looks a decade younger still."

Ellen smiled at a man obviously in love.

"Well, as long as the two of you are happy, maybe you can act out your own little stories."

"Ellen! Really!" Edwin blushed and looked around to make sure Marion wasn't nearby to hear.

"It's fine Edwin. I promise to behave for the rest of lunch."

Surprisingly, especially to Ellen, she did.

Edwin looked up as Mrs. Baxter walked into his office. His regular secretary had just left to care for a sister who had been injured in a car accident. Mrs. Baxter was actually the majordomo of the law firm, keeping the lights on and everything running smoothly. She still took time with every lawyer, however, to help make him think it was his idea to do things her way.

"There's a Mr. Wilcox from the DA's office on the phone for you. How long do you want me to keep him waiting?"

Edwin smiled, knowing the solidly built woman would push Wilcox off for a week if he wanted it. He had told the obnoxious lawyer with the DA about his meeting with Ellen on Wednesday morning, and was expecting the call.

"Put him through Mrs. Baxter. With any luck, it will be the last call he makes here for a long time." Edwin gave her thirty seconds and picked up the phone.

"Hello Tom."

"Did Ellen Patrick have anything useful to say yesterday or give you Edwin?"

Direct to the point and no tact, no wonder he was a lousy public defender.

"Not about a journal or anything. Are you certain that Owen had another set of notes?"

"There are gaps in some of his official records, and he was too thorough to allow that to happen."

"I know that, which is why I wish you'd let me look at the records again. You might not recognize some of his cross-references."

"Sorry Edwin, you gave up the privilege when you left the DA's office."

Of course if you hadn't, you'd probably be just as dead as Owen by now. Wilcox stared daggers into the phone. *Being almost as much an insufferable prig as he was.*

"Do you want me to ask again sometime?"

"Unless we find more gaps in Owen's calendar, there's no need to further upset her."

"You think so? She's always struck me as more stable than that."

"Please Edwin, she's just another debutante running around unencumbered by higher thoughts except to catch a husband."

He certainly doesn't know Ellen like he thinks he does.

"Fine then Tom. Can you at least tell me …" Edwin heard the clack as Wilcox ended the call.

"He's lucky his family could buy his way through law school. Too bad they didn't send him to charm school as well." Edwin began thinking about why Tom Wilcox was so insistent on tracing Owen's movements over three years ago, when there was a knock on his door.

"Got time for an out-of-work, hungry ex-actress?"

"Natalie!" Edwin rose quickly and met his fiancée at the door.

"Well Edwin, can you take me out for a late lunch?"

He looked at his watch. It was almost 2 o'clock and he had worked through the midday meal again.

"Tell you what, give me fifteen minutes and we'll sneak out for the entire afternoon."

"Bad day?" Natalie looked concerned.

"Don't worry, five minutes after we leave here, I'll forget all about it."

Carl greeted Ellen as she handed the valet her keys and carried her tennis bag inside.

"I'm glad you could join me Ellen. These are my only weekdays off until the summer break."

"Well then Carl, as soon as I change my shoes, I'll join you and we can play a set."

Once on the court, Ellen quickly found that Carl had retained his skills from college. Better still, once Ellen warmed up, he gave no indication of going easy on her just because they were on a date.

There's more to him than I thought! Let's see how much.

Ellen was able to surprise Carl on multiple occasions, taking two games herself. With her physical regimen needed to maintain the Domino Lady's skills, she was able to make Carl work for every point of the two he won. After his second, he waved for a time-out. They both agreed to call it a tie and then stepped away for lunch. The older couple waiting for them acidly pointed out their time was up three minutes ago.

"You have an excellent forehand Ellen! Anna didn't tell me you still kept in training."

"Thank you Carl. I play now and then, but this last year has been a bit busy for me." Ellen was happy to have worked up an appetite, and Carl was still just as charming as last week.

Not to mention most of my forehands have been punches and judo throws!

"So I hear." He noticed Ellen's puzzled look. "Michael mentioned that you were involved with CIVIC in having those crooked police officers arrested."

Ellen was startled for a moment, then remembered her name had been in the paper and Anna had asked about it.

"My role was much less than the *Times* made it out to be. I really did little more than attend a few meetings and pay for some coffee and snacks." Carl pulled out Ellen's chair once they arrived at their table.

"Even so Ellen, that's says a lot about you. Most people never seem to care about this city unless the problem punches them in the face personally."

Ellen blinked and Carl suddenly realized his mistake.

"Oh my God, Ellen, I'm so sorry! I didn't mean to imply…"

"It's fine Carl." She leaned across the table and took his left hand. "My Father had me collecting his notes, doing legal research, and occasionally working in soup kitchens when he thought I needed to be reminded of the responsibility of having more than the next person."

"Thank you Ellen, but I shouldn't have said what I did."

"Tell you what, buy me a Mimosa to go with lunch and we'll call it even."

"Done!"

That evening, Ellen looked over the map of the movie stars' homes she picked up with the magazines one last time. Then, almost leaping from her bed, she moved swiftly to the armoire that once belonged to her Father.

The young woman removed and dropped her dressing gown onto the sofa next it. Opening its doors, she looked at the familiar, white evening gown, removed it from the hangar, and with a long practiced movement, drew it over her head. A quick flip dropped it over her shoulders, a short tug pulled it down over the Kestos undergarment covering her ample chest, and a twist at her trim waist dropped it past her full hips, garter belt, and then down her trim legs to halt just above her stockinged feet.

Ellen quickly slipped on and buckled her T-Straps. The custom-made, Cuban heels were more comfortable than they appeared, allowed her to run, and stayed on even when she buried the heel in mud or, more often, a crook's instep.

To complete the costume and provide protection against the cold evening, she lifted a black cloak out of the closet, draped it over her shoulders, and secured the hidden clasp at her throat. Still hanging in the wardrobe were an identical dress and cloak, but with the colors reversed from the ones she was wearing. Ellen had worn them several times in her first few months as the Domino Lady, but now they hung mostly as a memory.

She left the hood down, and reached back to push two points on the back of the armoire. A panel opened and Ellen reached in to retrieve her mask, .22 pistol, the bag with the sapphire set, and a slim box containing a syringe and a vial of the knockout drug she used so effectively.

The box and mask each went into a separate pocket in the cloak while the .22 she slipped into a garter designed to hold the small automatic. At the last moment, she decided to take only the ring to Powell, so she wrapped it in a handkerchief and placed it in the same pocket as the mask. Ellen replaced the remaining pieces next to her Father's coded date book, the original occupant of the secret compartment, and closed the panel.

After the fiasco with the stolen roadster, Ellen decided to use her own auto for the trip to Powell's home. A quick switch with the license plate from a previous adventure and she was off.

You'd think people would get rid of these sliding glass, patio doors. They're too easy to open from the outside.

After another moment, the Domino Lady glided through the now open door, and into Powell's study. She didn't go upstairs, the last two years taught her that bringing the homeowner to her was far safer than actually sneaking up on someone. After a few minutes of banging items on the desk and rattling books in the bookcase, she heard footsteps come down the stairs and a switch being turned on.

The man who entered look much like his characters from the movies. A little older and grayer, Ellen thought, but that was no doubt the late hour and lack of makeup.

"Good evening Mr. Powell. I'm sorry to disturb you, but making a daytime appointment through a personal secretary is not something I usually do."

"I've read about you. The press calls you The Domino Lady." He gestured around the study. "I'm afraid you won't find much here, after several break-ins in the neighborhood, everything valuable and small enough I put into a safety deposit box."

"It may ruin my reputation, but I'm actually here to return something I found in another home Mr. Powell." She took a step forward and lifted her hand with the ring from under her cloak. "Here."

Powell looked like someone had just slapped him. "Where did you find it?" He whispered as he took the ring from her hand.

"I'd rather not say; just know that the woman I took it from is not going to report it to the Robbery Division."

Powell smiled at the ring for a moment, looked up at the daring woman in front of him, and gave her the grin that sent hearts racing in the movie theaters.

"Can you join me for a drink and tell me what you can say?"

"I'd be happy to Mr. Powell."

"Well then Miss Domino," He turned toward the door and held out an arm. "Let's go to the living room for a proper drink."

The Domino Lady took his arm and they began to walk.

"If you're happy now, wait till you taste my martinis."

"You were being modest. This may be the best martini I've ever drank!"

"I learned how to mix them for *The Thin Man*. Great bartender in a little seaside hotel up in Carmel taught me." Powell stared at the Domino for a moment and managed to look sad and happy at the same time.

"What is it Mr. Powell?"

"First off, you have to call me Bill now that I'm your bartender. Second, it's that dress you're wearing. You know what people started calling that style after *Dinner at Eight* was released back in '33 don't you?"

"No."

"A Jean Harlow."

Eyes widening behind the mask, she admitted, "I had forgotten about that."

"That's fine Miss Domino, you fill out that gown almost as well as she did."

It had been a long time since anyone has used the word almost when referring to the masked dare doll's physical assets. That charmed her even more than the martini.

I can see why Jean loved him so much.

"Thank you Bill."

"You're welcome. Now, you owe me a story." Powell moved to the sofa and patted the cushion next to him.

The Domino Lady smiled, sat down, and told Powell everything except for Agnes Victor's name and the exact streets she was racing down.

"Ha! Ha! Ha!" The actor laughed until he nearly cried. "I wish I could have been a passenger in that car chase! Either automobile!"

The Domino Lady took another sip of her martini and then asked, "Why wasn't it an engagement ring Bill?"

"Right to the point, huh?" Powell finished his own martini, took a cigarette from the box on the end table, looked at it, put it back, and then replied, "It should have been. I was originally looking for a ruby necklace, but then I saw that ring." Powell laughed and continued. "Myrna Loy said it was the gaudiest thing she had ever seen that didn't come out of a Woolworth."

The Domino Lady almost blushed to hear her own words but kept her composure.

"So how do you think it disappeared ...?"

She stopped mid-question and they both turned at the sound of breaking glass. Then she moved quickly into the hallway with Powell a step behind her.

"Friends of yours?"

"No Bill, I work alone. Makes it much easier to divide the loot." Listening to the other sounds, she shook her head. "Breaking in through the kitchen is never smart. Sounds echo much too loud."

"Do me a favor Miss Domino and let's slide back into the study to call the police."

She was a little disappointed Powell didn't pull a gun out of his robe, then laughed to herself over acting like a fan.

"Operator, this is William Powell. Yes, that William Powell. I need you to send the police to my home at ... You already know the address? Well of course you do. Yes, send them over now, I don't think the bad men are going to wait patiently. Thank you."

"OK." He put the phone down. "That was my civic duty." The actor opened a desk drawer and pulled out a .38. "Now let's see what they have to say for themselves."

"Sounds good to me Bill." She lifted the .22 out from under her cloak.

Powell chuckled. "Don't tell me where it was, my imagination is going to have too much fun figuring it out."

They walked into the hallway to find the two burglars just leaving the kitchen. One had a recently broken nose while the other one barely had a chin. Powell pulled the hammer back on the .38 and pointed it between the two.

"You boys broke into the wrong home."

"Naw, the broad we want is right behind you."

Powell moved the pistol to the left and sighted directly on Broken Nose.

"Speak kindly to my guest or I'll give you a third nostril."

The smaller thug tugged at the sleeve of the other one.

"Come on Scotty. We're getting paid to slap around a twist, not play stare down with a .38."

"All right Weed." He looked at Powell and nodded his head respectfully. "That hand ain't twitched a bit. Maybe there's more to you than just a couple of acting lessons Mr. Powell."

"It helps when I've got you cold and flat-footed."

The bigger thug grinned at that.

"Come on Weed. Let's go."

"Hold on." Powell said, "Miss Domino, they were here for you. If you like, I can hold them for the police while you leave and then just keep your name out of it."

"I appreciate that Bill, but what I need is to find out why they want to see me."

"You heard the lady, boys. Start talking."

"I ain't saying nothing, and neither is he." Scotty jabbed a thumb at Weed.

"How about a bargain then?" The Domino Lady stepped forward and dropped the .22 back under her cloak. Out of sight, she secured it to the garter.

"We go out onto Mr. Powell's patio and see who puts who on the ground. If I win, you tell me why you're here. If you win, you get to leave and Bill tells the cops it was a couple of fans looking for an autograph."

"What if I decide I want that ring anyway?"

Powell spoke up. "Then I shoot your friend here in a very delicate place." He pointed the gun at Scotty. "And then I put the rest in you."

"I guess I can live with that." The big thug replied.

"Don't speak for me!" Weed jumped in.

"What's wrong Weed? Don't you trust your friend to fight a girl?" At the last word, the Domino Lady unhooked the hidden clasp and flipped her cloak to hang over her left arm. Fortunately, she was standing slightly behind Powell so the actor didn't lose focus.

"I even promise not to hit you in the nose."

Realizing that the police would soon arrive, Powell called the operator from the patio and had her connect him with the nightshift watch commander. He assured the man that tomorrow morning would be fine. The perpetrators ran off, tripping over their feet like the autograph hounds they most certainly had to be, when he turned on the lawn sprinkler.

That taken care of, Scotty took off his jacket and handed it to Weed. The smaller man carefully folded and laid it across the back of one of the deck chairs.

"You sure you want to do this Scotty? We can just track her down some other time."

"Knock that off Weed!" He looked back at the Domino Lady. "I haven't backed down from a fight since I was ten years old, and I'm not letting some frail get the better of me."

"Think about it Scotty! She don't move like some damsel in distress, and she was holding that .22 steady as a rock before. She gets a thumb in your eye, it ain't gonna matter how tough you are."

"That's enough out of you." Powell declared. "If the combatants are ready, let's get this soiree started."

Despite the potential danger if the big thug did manage to land a blow, the Domino Lady could feel the smile spread across her face as she adjusted her footing. Judo training here and in the Orient made her much more dangerous than many men thought possible.

Scotty tried to grab for her curls and looked at his hand in surprise when he came up empty. He was even more surprised when he felt the crushing blow on his left instep and howled in pain.

"Augh!" As he limped backward, the Domino Lady grabbed his still outstretched left hand, turned it upside down and pulled him forward. The sudden shift to his injured foot elicited another howl as the blonde marvel threw Scotty across the patio to land on top of the table.

The loud crack of the breaking glass made everyone jump. Weed started feeling his chest, thinking Powell had pulled the trigger. With a sigh of relief, he dropped his hands back to his sides.

"Want to give up Scotty? The next time, I'll probably put you right through the table."

Scotty carefully lifted himself off the table and then checked his face and chest.

"Nah!" He grinned. "I haven't had this much fun in a long time!" He moved toward the Domino Lady again, this time with his hands folded up. He moved in cautiously, but the masked beauty didn't move except to turn her head as he circled to his left.

Once he was only in her peripheral vision, she turned slightly to her right and assumed an Age-uke, or Rising Block; almost too late. The Domino Lady barely moved Scotty's strike quickly enough to take only a glancing blow off the right side of her skull, rather than on her perfectly shaped jaw-line. She shook her shoulders to help work off the shock and then smiled at Scotty.

"Well, you're a bit faster than I thought. This may take longer than another minute or two."

"You ain't so bad yourself." Scotty replied grudgingly.

They continued to strike and block for long enough, that Powell and Weed each took up a chair and watched like it was a prize fight at the Olympic Auditorium.

"Care to place a wager Mr. Weed?"

"No thanks Mr. Powell. I don't think I'd collect, and Scotty'd be real mad if I bet against him."

The blonde marvel knew she was breathing hard and sweating harder. She was also tasting blood when Scotty hit hard enough that she bit both cheeks.

At least Scotty looks worse than me! She thought, but realized she had to finish this quickly. Once she dodged the next attack, she pretended to turn badly on her left foot, but recovered immediately, showing only the barest hint of a limp.

As she hoped, Scotty pressed instantly on what he thought was an advantage. She moved immediately off the uninjured ankle, turned and caught his left arm as the right overextended. With Scotty completely off-balanced, the Domino Lady forced his left arm behind his back and pushed him off his feet to land hard enough on the patio to knock the wind out of him.

Trying to catch his breath, Scotty felt a tug at his back pocket and looked up just in time to see his own sap come swinging down, but it tapped the top of his head just hard enough to make him wince.

"Oh, this is a nice one." The Domino Lady looked appreciatively at the leather wrapped, lead shot in her left hand and smiled at the smaller thug. "I think I'll keep it." Then she smacked it into her right palm with a loud crack.

Weed did the only smart thing possible and started to talk. Scotty sat on the patio, rubbing his head.

"After you stole that ring from our boss, she figured that you'd …"

"Wait a minute." The Domino Lady interrupted, "The fishwife is your boss, not her husband?"

"Well yeah, her brother is pretty high up in the rackets around here."

"Who is her brother?"

"Marvin Green. He and Agnes work the angles to get a piece of the studio's pie."

"How does her husband fit into it?"

"He's on the committee that approves the studios getting film permits in the city. Since he knows where everyone is going, Marvin has a leg up on roach coaches and hauling out garbage."

"Roach coaches?" The Domino Lady looked at Powell.

"The food trucks that provide the meals whenever we shoot on location; that's outside a studio." Powell looked back to Weed as Scotty finally got to his feet and sat in a deck chair.

"How did the Victors, either of them, get Jean's ring?"

"We don't know." Scotty spoke up. He had moved down from his head to his ribs. "That's some of that Judo stuff right?"

"Yes." The Domino Lady replied, "How did you like it?"

"I didn't, but I think I need to learn some more about it."

After a few more questions about the Victor's personal habits, the blonde marvel was almost ready to let them go.

"One more question, who exactly do you work for? The fishwife or her brother?"

"We get paid by the studio. They loan us out to guys like Victor when it's related."

"Who does the loaning?"

Powell interrupted. "I know who it is Miss Domino." He didn't sound pleased about it.

"Do you think they were involved?"

"Probably not, but this is one of the reasons why actors don't trust the studios and when we have enough money to afford it, we hire our own lawyers and accountants."

Scotty and Weed sat quietly waiting.

"Are you happy for now Miss Domino?"

"That's some of that Judo stuff right?"

"I can't think of anything else to ask Bill. Weed and Scotty held up their end of the bargain. Besides, if I need more information, I'm certain I can find them again with not much effort."

Weed looked relieved, but Scotty was fairly certain he'd just been insulted.

"You heard Miss Domino, boys. Amscray."

After they departed, Powell looked at the Domino Lady and put on his best 'Nick Charles' face.

"Got time for some first aid and another martini gorgeous?"

"It would be my pleasure. As long as you tell me more about Jean."

"I'm sorry Bill. I should have just sent you the ring in the mail."

"Perhaps, but those two would have showed up here anyway, and I haven't had this much fun since before Jean passed." Powell poured them each another martini and then dropped a pearl onion in each one so smoothly, they barely rippled the surface. Fortunately, his first aid efforts didn't need to include dressing split lips and the only bruise forming at the moment was above her hairline.

"You've told me your tale and got to hear Jean's story, well now I want to find out the story of this ring." Powell gave his most roguish look. "Care to join me?"

Well, Colonel Mayfield did say to get involved in a few things not related to Dad's death.

"I'm in Bill!"

"So now what Miss Domino?"

"Beating the bushes, strong-arming cheap hoods, and lots of questions."

"Let me guess, the first one is where did I buy that ring?"

"It's the place to start. Just tell me where it is and I ..."

"Oh no! You can come with me, but I want to look the jeweler in the eye and have him explain why that ring is so important that two thugs came to my house and make me believe he had nothing to do with it."

Domino gestured to her dress. "I'm not attired for an afternoon stroll."

"Well then, how do you feel about disguises?"

The young avenger grinned from ear to ear.

"I have the perfect outfit for jewelry shopping!"

"Well then, when would you like to go?"

"I suppose tomorrow is out of the question, but Saturday should be fine."

Powell waved his hand at her. "Never fear Kitten! Nick Charles can open any door, but William Powell has the jeweler's home phone number. Would 11 o'clock be good? We can have a nice lunch afterward."

The Domino Lady laughed gaily and continued sipping her martini as Powell looked up the number to call.

Ellen met Bill in front of the jewelry store at exactly five minutes before 11 o'clock.

"If I didn't already know it was you Miss Domino, I'd never have guessed it."

Ellen smiled at the compliment, but resisted the urge to wink at Powell over her large sunglasses. She couldn't wear her mask underneath them on Rodeo Drive like she could in other parts of Los Angeles.

"You can't tell my chestnut hair isn't the real thing?"

"No, but to be honest, the dress does distract just a bit from your overall appearance."

Ellen smiled at the compliment. The dress was one of several designed for exactly that reaction. The cloth was a conservative print that would not draw attention from a distance, but the cut was just tight enough in the right places to distract close observers from important details, like her dimpled chin and sharp cheekbones.

Not that she had to worry about it while standing next to William Powell. His Navy sport coat complimented his tan trousers perfectly. His slightly lighter blue tie popped against his crisp, white shirt and perfectly matched the band on his Panama hat. Somehow, he found a perfectly shaped, yellow rose as a boutonnière.

"So what do I call you while you're in this disguise?"

"Let's make it Winnie, Bill."

"Winnie, huh?" Powell smiled at her. "I guess that'll do." He put out his arm. "Are you ready to go jewelry shopping Winnie?"

"Let's!"

Ellen already knew where they were going, but she still found herself holding her breath as they walked in the store. Hudson Winthrop not only sold some of the finest jewelry in Hollywood, but actresses actively sought him out when they needed something spectacular for the red carpet at their latest movie premiere or a high-profile charity event. His employees all looked like they were from central casting and a few of the young men and women obviously had training as they modeled a watch or a pair of earrings.

Powell asked the young lady who approached them to let Mr. Winthrop know Bill Powell and friend were here. A few moments later, she came back and asked them to follow her to the private showing room.

Hudson himself looked a bit like Lionel Barrymore in a courtroom setting. As they entered the private room, Bill held up the ring.

"Mr. Powell! You found it!"

"Yes Hudson. The story behind getting it back may just curl your toes."

"May I?" The jewelry held his hands out. Powell nodded and placed it in his palm.

"I could not find a lady's setting large enough to hold this beauty, so I had one made." Without taking his eyes off the ring, Winthrop smiled as he remembered. "It spoke to me, so I had to do it."

He looked up at Powell with no change in expression. "Does it fit the young lady, or do I need to make an adjustment?"

"Oh no." Ellen interjected, "I found the ring and returned it to Bill. If I want something sparkly, I'll buy it for myself." *Probably not here however.* She thought.

"Hudson, I didn't ask at the time, but I am now. Where exactly did you get that beauty?" Powell asked.

The jeweler handed the ring back to Powell and wistfully looked at him.

"It was a purchase from a seller out of Siam and Cambodia. He shows up every two years with mostly decent stones, but there are always a few spectacular ones."

Ellen noticed an odd look crossed his face.

"Was there something wrong with the stone or your seller?"

"Well, not really but …"

"Come on Hudson. It could be important."

"This sapphire had been cut already when he brought it to me Mr. Powell. More carefully than just by a cutter looking to expand his profit. Someone very skilled, but they had used very primitive tools." He looked over at Ellen. "You can tell by the edges if someone is using modern, precision tools, or a set from over a century ago; softer metals, no diamond cutting tips, that sort of thing."

"How many where there?" Ellen asked.

"Four sapphires, three rubies, and a handful of lesser stones."

Powell realized where Ellen was heading and jumped in.

"What happened to the other sapphires?"

"Well, they were much smaller than the one I used for Jean's ring, so I had my cutter split the larger stone for a pair of earrings and the smaller stones I turned into a brooch."

"Who bought them?" Powell.

"I'll have to look it up." Hudson got up to go into his office. He returned in less than five minutes.

"The brooch and earrings were both bought by Reuben Victor. He's a local councilman." Hudson looked at Domino's sudden glance at Powell.

"That's a familiar name I'm guessing."

"I'm more familiar with his wife." Ellen leaned back against the sofa she sat on, and then picked up her purse and removed the matching pieces.

"I should have told you last night Bill, but I wasn't certain if they also belonged to you or if they were stolen from someone else."

Once she laid them on the coffee table, Hudson immediately arranged them on a display tray with the ring.

"That's fine Winnie." Powell looked up at the jeweler. "Why didn't you sell me the full set?"

"I finished the ring first, and had just put it out in the case to see how it looked. You walked in almost as I slid the glass shut. When you told me who it was for, I knew it belonged with Miss Harlow."

Bill suddenly grew very grim. "Then whoever took it had to have known about the matching pieces or had already bought them."

Hudson gasped. "Was it Reuben Victor's wife who stole the ring? How did she get it? Was it in their home?"

"Easy Hudson!" Bill quickly brightened, then reached over and patted the man's forearm. "No one said anything about theft or breaking and entering." He quickly winked at Ellen and then turned back to the jeweler. "Let's keep it that way for now, all right?"

"Of course, Mr. Powell. As a matter of fact, I haven't seen Miss Harlow's ring since you purchased it."

"That's the boy, Hudson!"

They all got up, shook hands and departed the store. Once outside, Powell turned to Ellen immediately.

"So when do we confront Reuben or do you want to go back to the beginning?"

Ellen laughed. "I am not going to Siam, Bill. That's a mystery for another day."

"OK then Winnie. Now, let's go have lunch and talk about what to do with Reuben Victor. There's a place I like nearby and someone I want you to meet."

A few minutes later, Ellen was sitting at a very nice café just far enough off the beaten path that no photographers were present.

"So who am I meeting Bill?"

"A rather exceptional woman who comes highly recommended as an investigator and all round go-to-gal for us shiftless Hollywood types."

"She sounds interesting. Are you looking to replace me already?"

"Ha! No Winnie, just myself. I'm already tired out for the day and we've only had time for a single mimosa so far."

Ellen reached out and put a hand on Powell's arm. "Is it the radium treatments?"

"Yes. I'd love to follow every clue and wrestle every crook, but I'm not up for that quite yet." Powell looked over and waved at someone to join them. "I think you'll like her."

Ellen looked up and nearly choked on her mimosa. The dark-haired woman standing in front of her was very familiar.

"Hello Winnie! Long time no see!"

Powell looked at Ellen with surprise. "You know Sandra Elliot already?"

"Winnie and I are old friends, Mr. Powell. Of course the last time I saw her, she was driving off with my boyfriend."

Ellen stared at the familiar face and found herself almost speechless. It had been two months since she met Sandra while working to bring down a group of corrupt police officers that might have been tied to her Father's death.

"Why Sandra, how marvelous to see you! I understand you're joining us today."

"Since Mr. Powell is already paying for my time, why not?" Sandra dropped into the chair across from Ellen. The dark-haired woman was wearing a tailored pantsuit, similar to the one Ellen wore to Anna's dinner, but the jacket was looser around the waist than was considered fashionable.

She's got a sap or a gun under there. Ellen thought to herself. Sandra had nothing to do with the criminals she was chasing, but as a driver, mechanic, and fighter, Ellen's interest was piqued enough by the other woman to try and find out more.

After the end of that adventure, Ellen looked for Sandra out of curiosity, but found more questions than answers. The only trace Ellen discovered of her was a one-room, furnished apartment in a women's residence hotel. It had been rented for just three months under the name of Sandra Baker.

"Still pretending to race cars?" Sandra asked.

"I race them just fine." Ellen replied. "It's the Highway Patrol that doesn't like me showing off."

"Twisty moped around for almost two weeks after you disappeared."

"You mean after I disappeared with Rex Mays' car. He was more interested in that racer than he ever was in me."

"Fair enough." Sandra looked over at the actor and jumped in before he could say anything.

"This will not be a problem Mr. Powell. Winnie here walked into the middle of a case I was working on for another client. Her actions had no effect on the outcome however and we parted with no ill will."

"That's not entirely accurate Sandra dear." Ellen dryly commented.

"I'm so sorry, does your jaw still hurt?"

"No more than your arm, I'm sure."

"I think I'm going to want several drinks." Powell commented and began rubbing his hands together. "This is beginning to look like a very interesting lunch!"

"Wow." Sandra looked stunned as Ellen and Powell finished their story. Lunch had been served, eaten, and they were waiting for the coffee.

"Are you certain Mr. Winthrop is being forthright Sir?"

"Yes Sandra. I've known Hudson for a number of years, and he had no reason to lie to me about this."

"How about you Winnie?"

"I agree with Bill. Winthrop was almost hypnotized by the ring when he saw it and started speaking immediately. I don't think he had time to come up with a lie."

"Well then," Sandra stood up. "We need to need to pay a visit to Mrs. Victor and her husband."

Powell stretched and yawned. "You'll have to do it without me. I need to rest and then I have an early call tomorrow for studio publicity pictures."

"OK Bill." Ellen turned to Sandra and put her hand out. "Truce?"

"Truce." Sandra replied and shook hands. The two of them promised the actor a complete report as long as he rested up as long as possible.

"OK then, I'll head home and wait for you like Nero waits for Archie." He got up, received a handshake from Sandra and a buss on the cheek from Ellen, then left for his car.

The two women watched Powell depart for a moment, and then sat down again as the waiter brought their coffee, smoothly removed the place setting already set up for Powell, and departed with barely a breeze in the air.

"If it was anyone else, Winnie, I'd be suspicious of her motives in getting this close to a client."

"Why do you say that?"

"Because of what happened to Twisty."

"What do you mean?"

"The Domino Lady could have hung him out to dry with his boss. Instead, she made certain to point out that Twisty was just out of his league with her; well, you I should say."

Ellen warmed to the unusual compliment.

"I might have need or use of Twisty again sometime." Ellen shook her head. "It made no sense to get rid of someone that high up after just one little B&E."

"Fair enough." Sandra sipped her coffee a bit longer and then looked at Ellen.

"Is your car nearby?"

"Close enough."

"Want to park it nearby and then take mine over to the Victor's home so we don't stand out quite so much?"

"Is it the same Coupe I saw before?"

"Absolutely!"

"Can I drive?" Ellen coyly asked.

"Only if I'm shot, unconscious, and you have to drive me to the nearest hospital."

"Sandra darling, it's a deal!"

"Now what?" Ellen and Sandra asked at the same time. There was a sedan and one of the new model Plymouth station wagons parked outside the Victor's front door, with a trailer attached to the Plymouth. As the women watched from the curb, Councilman and Mrs. Victor left the home, got into the sedan and departed with the station wagon and two highway patrol officers inside after them.

"The one driving the sedan is the officer I helped crashed last week."

Sandra reached behind the seat and grabbed a clipboard. Next, she pulled a pair of glasses and a soft hat from the glove compartment.

"Let's see if the Victors like giving to charity, Winnie."

In a few minutes, Sandra returned with the knowledge that the Victors would be gone camping for three days.

"Even better, the household staff goes home every afternoon when the Victors are gone." Both women decided to keep the truce intact over dinner. To Ellen's surprise, Sandra chose one of the nicer restaurants in the area and offered to pay.

They were seated quickly and the waiter took their drink order immediately.

"OK Sandra, what's the story here?"

The brunette woman replied with a totally straight face.

"I'm a private investigator working for the FBI and certain private clients who need to maintain anonymity."

Ellen couldn't help but laugh, and Sandra even chuckled herself.

"I know, it still sounds ridiculous to me too, and I've been doing this for over two years now."

"You're serious!" Ellen exclaimed.

"Since October 1935." Sandra responded.

"May 1936 for me." Ellen said.

"May? The first report Turner has on you is July …" Sandra stopped suddenly and closed her eyes.

"Oh my Sandra! Who in the world is Mr. Turner? Or should I say Agent Turner?"

"He's my boss when I do work for the FBI." Sandra shook her head ruefully. "Don't spread that name around, OK? He's got his neck on the line every time he puts me to work as it is."

"I'm OK if you can keep the month of May to yourself?"

"It's a deal Winnie."

"So what does that make you Sandra? A G-Woman? A G-Girl?"

"No, I'm not technically an FBI agent. Back in the '20s, there was Alaska Davidson. She served two years before Hoover asked for her resignation in 1924. She died back in '34."

"She must have been quite a woman."

"I got to know her a couple of years before she died, when I was turning wrenches full time."

"How did you manage that?"

"Her maiden name is Packard. Sound familiar?"

"Her family started the company?"

"Yes, her two brothers." Sandra smiled at the memory of meeting Alaska and continued. "Eventually, she told me about her time in the Bureau, and here I am. I'm what Agent Turner calls an independent contractor."

The waiter came with their drinks and took both their orders. The two women traded small talk and both agreed that *Bringing Up Baby* was a nice comedy, but not Grant or Hepburn's best work.

"This restaurant looks a bit outside your usual price range Sandra."

"I'd say the same about you Winnie, but I'm starting to think you're used to having people wait on you."

"I've had men waiting on me since I was fourteen Sandra. Were you a late bloomer?"

"Ha, ha." Sandra tossed back the rest of her drink and put the glass back on the table without a sound. "Maybe we better stick to movies until after dinner."

An hour later, both women had finished their meals, sorbet for dessert, and were friends again by the time their coffee arrived. Ellen quizzed Sandra further about her career choice.

"So no badge?"

"Yes, but the pay is a lot better as a contractor. I make as much as the men and Hoover even pays for my bullets."

"What about that beautiful Coupe?"

"Oh no Winnie! That baby is all mine; lock, stock, and title!"

"You're lucky, Rex Mays literally went over his car with a magnifying glass when I returned it."

"So would I if some dizzy broad went driving off with my little girl!" Sandra leaned forward and put her chin in her right hand. "So how did you get Mays' car?"

Ellen told her about 90% of the truth. She left out Roger McKane's name, her own involvement in stealing a different one of Mays' racers a year earlier, and the name of her Father in teaching her to drive.

"That's quite a tale Winnie. How much is true?"

"More than enough to keep it interesting."

"OK then, what do you think about going back to the Victor's home tomorrow?"

"Strike while the iron is hot?"

"More like flooring the accelerator on a clear, open road."

Since this was a nighttime visit, the Domino Lady arrived in her 'Harlow' with driving jacket over it. She met Sandra on the street behind and below the Victor's home, and put on her mask as the brunette got out of her Coupe and moved into the roadster.

"The house across the street is empty. Park there."

"This isn't my first B&E, Sandra. I drove down their street before I came here."

They entered the home through the attached changing room that led to the backyard pool. As they entered the home, the smell of chlorine was quickly replaced by another odor familiar to both young women.

They found the bodies in the kitchen, every wine bottle smashed and the rack empty. The highway patrolman looked like he was asleep, except for the bloody mess that used to be the back of his skull. The blow was a complete surprise, his weapon still holstered.

Mrs. Victor did not look like she was asleep. Whoever killed her made certain she saw it coming. The blows to her face stayed away from her eyes so she missed nothing.

Despite the last two years, Ellen was still horrified by what she saw. Sandra looked equally ill at the sight in front of her.

"Who did this?" Sandra whispered. "I've seen some awful beatings before, but never a woman like this." Sandra got down closer. "It looks like both of her cheekbones are broken."

"It was someone close to at least one of them, probably Mrs. Victor."

"How do you figure?"

"Experience." The Domino Lady replied. "Whenever I've seen someone beaten this badly, it's almost always been done by someone close to them." She took a deep breath. "I've run into a couple of so-called 'professional killers', and none of them would do this. They'd call it sloppy and careless."

Sandra shook her head and looked over at Ellen. "My experience tells me to leave immediately, and look out the windows before heading out the front door."

"I couldn't agree more Sandra. Let's go."

As they drove back to Powell's home, Ellen said it first.

"Victor Reuben. It had to be him."

"Now I have to figure out what to do about him."

Ellen looked at the other woman. "What are you going to do? Turn him

Ellen was still horrified by what she saw. Sandra looked equally ill.

over to the police?"

"I have personal knowledge of a prime suspect's motive in a double murder Winnie. What do you expect me to do?"

"I want to talk to him first. Find out why he sent those two thugs over to Powell's home and why Harlow's ring is so important to him."

When they returned, Powell was more exhausted than when they left him.

"Bill, you promised to rest."

"I did Miss Domino. The doctor told me to expect a few days like this after each treatment. They don't always come at the same time."

"If this is the case Mr. Powell, then we need to put confronting Reuben Victor on hold until you're back on your feet."

Powell nodded in agreement. "Absolutely Sandra. I want to be there when you question him."

"Now Bill, be reasonable."

"Not where this is concerned. I'll wait for a few days, but if you come back and tell me that you braced him without me there, I'll simply find out when he's at the studio next and use him for target practice."

Frustrated, the Domino Lady looked to Sandra.

"You know him better than I do. Is he serious?"

"I think so Winnie. He's really not..."

The phone ringing interrupted them. The Domino Lady was closer, and moved to grab it, but then they heard the housekeeper pick up the extension in the hallway. After a few moments, she knocked on the bedroom door.

"There's a call for you Miss Elliot."

"The only person who would know to call me here is Turner. Excuse me."

The Domino Lady squeezed Powell's hand and then walked down to his study. Once inside, she looked over the actor's selection of Whiskey and blended Scotch. A quick search turned up Orgeat and lemons. A few minutes later, she had a Cameron's Kick ready for herself and one for Sandra.

"Good news?" The Domino Lady asked as Sandra walked into the study.

"For me yes, maybe not for you and Mr. Powell." Sandra took the cocktail and drank half of it.

"A lead on an FBI case just got hot. Turner wants me to come in for a briefing in the morning and then drive up to Sacramento." Sandra looked at the Domino Lady. "You asked before if Powell was serious. He is, and you have to try and keep him resting until I get back."

"I'll do everything I can to keep Bill away from Reuben Victor until then Sandra."

With Reuben Victor on hold, Ellen returned home to rest and catch up on her own life. The next morning, she had Marion prepare lunch and then sent her off on errands that would take most of the day. With the housekeeper gone, Ellen had time to fully meditate and then engage in an extensive workout. With no training partner, she concentrated on her Atemi-waza and Uke-waza or body-striking and blocking techniques.

The recent tennis match with Carl reminded her that she needed to stretch more than just the muscles needed to throw or punch an opponent, so Ellen stretched and performed the same calisthenics routine she did at Berkeley as part of her tennis training. Almost two hours later, Ellen felt better than she had in weeks. As she toweled off her face and neck, Ellen suddenly realized that she had not stretched her mental abilities as much as she should either.

"Let's see, Edwin said three and a half years ago at Seal Beach. Dad's datebook went back nearly two years, so the meeting should be there; as long as I can determine which one it is, of course."

The lithe, young woman took a quick, hot shower to soothe her muscle aches, then wrapped herself in a robe and her hair in a towel. Taking the datebook out of the armoire, she sat on one end of the bedroom sofa with her feet up on the opposite arm. She opened a pad for notes and began looking for what she hoped would be the right date while sipping a lemonade.

"All right now, the names in the book are always related in some fashion to their real counterpart, as are the subjects. I just need to figure out who and what."

She started by writing down the names and subjects in the datebook for the months of September and October of 1934. Then she tried using synonyms and antonyms to tie them to a subject she could remember her Father talking about back then. The problem was that she was in class in Berkeley by then and only spoke to Owen on weekends.

After thirty minutes of staring at the two columns and dozens of possibilities, Ellen had an inspiration. She leaped off the sofa, quickly grabbed the phone on her nightstand, and dialed the number Edwin gave her before he departed after lunch.

"Hello, Edwin? I kept thinking about our visit, and I thought of something Dad said once. I was home for a three-day weekend and he was leaving for a meeting. He was heading for Signal Hill. I know, because he was looking at a city map the night before. The funny thing is, when I asked him where he was going, he said if the office called, he was interviewing a witness in Seal Beach."

"Was there anything else Ellen?"

"That's why I called, I wondered if you might have time for dinner. Perhaps we can compare memories and it would also give me a chance to meet Natalie, if that's all right."

"I think she would like that. Perhaps I can help put any questions you have to rest and show my old office there really is nothing left to chew over." The line went quiet for a moment. "As a matter of fact, tonight is open. I've told Natalie so much about Owen, I think she will be thrilled to meet you."

Ellen was pleased with Edwin's restaurant selection. It was one her Father had taken her to on several occasions and the atmosphere was still as friendly and the prime rib as tender as she remembered. She was also happy to see that Natalie wasn't instantly suspicious or jealous of her appearance. It was rare, so Ellen appreciated it all the more.

They kept the conversation to small talk over dinner. After ordering dessert, they moved to the outside area and Edwin switched to business.

"So what did you want to compare tonight Ellen?"

As the young woman choked back laughter, Natalie leaned in to whisper in Edwin's ear about his choice of words. He quickly blushed to his hairline and stammered an apology.

"It's fine Edwin. I know what you meant, of course." She leaned across the table, and with a glance to Natalie, patted him once on the hand.

"Now, I don't recall any names really, but Dad did occasionally talk about some of types of crimes he dealt with." Ellen leaned back and flashed a smile at Natalie. "He tried to keep it tame, but every now and then, he'd let slip with a juicy murder case or something involving one of the movie studios."

After an hour, Ellen told Edwin everything she could remember from three years ago. She committed to memory everything Edwin responded with so she could write it down later.

"Does any of this help Edwin?"

"I'm not certain Ellen. I can pass this back to the D.A.'s office for them to chew over."

"Who are you working with anyway?" Ellen asked.

Edwin hesitated, but Natalie jumped in.

"Oh tell her it was Tom Wilcox already Edwin."

"Natalie, you know I can't tell anyone …" The middle-aged attorney quickly closed his mouth, realizing she had just answered Ellen's question anyway and smiled ruefully.

"Since I have apparently been outfoxed, I'll go to the bar and get us another round of drinks."

As Edwin walked to the patio bar near them, Ellen and Natalie listened to the radio playing from inside the restaurant. After the song ended, the news came on.

"Police are now searching for the masked criminal known as the Domino Lady. According to Chief Davis, she is a suspect in the murders of Councilman Reuben Victor's wife, Agnes and Highway Patrol Officer Stanley Harris. While there is no confirmation for it, sources inside the Police Department say the daring, young thief and murder suspect left one of her black calling cards at the scene."

Ellen felt her blood run cold and her shoulders shook. Natalie noticed and reached over to take her hand.

"Are you all right Ellen? Do you want to move inside?"

"No, it was just the night breeze. I am feeling a bit tired though, would you mind terribly if I went home after we finish this drink?"

"Of course not." Natalie turned to Edwin as he set down the glasses. "We can finish our trip down memory lane some other time darling."

"Absolutely dear." Edwin looked to Ellen. "How does another dinner in a few weeks sound?"

"It sounds perfect Edwin. Why don't we make at my home?"

Two days later, Sandra returned. She was smiling, but refused to give any details; saying only that a little girl was no longer missing her Mommy and Daddy.

Powell had a schedule of Reuben Victor's schedule for meetings with the studio. A conversation with an executive's secretary got him the information on what day Victor was arriving alone. On those days he was granted access to a sound stage where filming was taking place. When he did finally go home, it would be by himself.

All they had to do was wait for him, and perhaps lock up the cook in the pantry for a few hours. Five minutes after they arrived and one very confused Armenian cook later, she was in the pantry with a warning to be quiet and an open bottle of Chablis to help her out with that.

"Sandra," Powell began, "Why don't you wait out front? Reuben doesn't know you're involved in this, so why not keep it that way if we can?"

The Domino Lady jumped in. "I promise to keep him out of trouble Sandra."

"Fine then, it's not like he can sneak up behind you."

"I can guess why you're here you little twist." Victor turned toward Powell. "What about you Powell?"

"Don't play games Reuben. You know we're here for the same reason."

"I don't think either of you know the serious trouble I can drop on the two of you."

"Sorry Councilman Victor, but it's hard to take a man seriously when he's named after Dan Reid's horse." The Domino Lady smiled at the Councilman's sudden snarl. "Now tell me how you got hold of Jean Harlow's ring."

"You'll have to ask Agnes." Reuben snapped his fingers. "No wait, you already killed her."

Powell responded by thumbing back the hammer on his .38 and pointed it at Reuben's nose.

"Answer the question. How did you get Jean's ring?" The look in Powell's eyes finally made the councilman begin to sweat.

"I walked on set right after the ambulance arrived. I stayed out of everyone's way and then just walked into her dressing room like I was invited."

"You saw the ring and recognized the design from Winthrop's, just like the earrings and brooch."

"Agnes had been after me to get it ever since she learned about it after we bought the others."

"So you just helped yourself."

"Why not? Agnes didn't like it that she couldn't wear it outside the house, but she was happy to get it anyway."

"You didn't know Jean wasn't coming out of the hospital when you took it though."

Reuben just sneered. "I don't see what the fuss is about now. Harlow's been dead for a year."

Before the Domino Lady could reach him, Powell lowered the hammer on the .38 and viciously slashed Victor across the face, driving him to his knees.

"Nine months." Powell said, then grabbed Victor by the ear and dragged him out onto the lanai. The councilman howled, but the actor pulled with a strength he hadn't felt since Jean died.

"It doesn't even feel like that. Do you have any idea what it's like to watch a young woman like Jean die like that?!" He raised the gun to strike Victor again, but the rush he felt was already beginning to fade.

"Bill!" The blonde bombshell rushed to his side and this time grabbed his arm, but Powell lowered it without a fight. He reversed the .38 in his hand, handed it over, and then waved her off.

"Forget him Miss Domino. I just lost my temper for a moment and forgot how much the radium treatments take it out of me." He sat down on a patio chair. "I should have expected that comment out of a mutt that would kill his own wife."

"Let's go. If the police don't haul Victor in, his former brother-in-law will take care of him."

Reuben suddenly sat up. "What are you talking about? What does Marvin know?"

They turned around and headed for the front door.

"I'll end your career you bastard! No film you're on will ever get another permit to film in L.A.!" Victor came out holding a cloth to his cheek and temple.

Powell ignored him, but the Domino Lady turned her head to look back, and caught a glint off metal just in time to shove Powell toward Sandra who had jumped out of the car when Reuben Victor came out yelling.

"Do you hear me? I'll put you and that thieving bimbo …" RATA-TAT-TAT-TAT! Sudden gunfire knocked the councilman back against the doorframe and as he slumped to the ground, Sandra pulled Powell down to the ground behind the car and covered him with her own body. As the black sedan pulled away on squealing tires, the masked blonde took aim and put three rounds from her .22 into the rear window.

"Bill!" The Domino Lady looked over to see Powell looking very pale and almost unconscious. He waved weakly at her.

"I'm not hurt, just tired and sick."

The doctor removed his stethoscope from Powell's chest and looked at the blood pressure number his nurse had written down on the chart. He shook his head and then locked eyes with his patient.

"You'll be fine Bill, but you have to stop and let the effects of the radium run their course. The more you exert yourself, the longer your recovery is going to be and you will NOT come back one hundred percent if you keep this up." He poked Powell in the chest as he said 'not' and then got up from the edge of Powell's bed and reached for his tweed jacket. As Doctor Wilde slipped it on, his nurse began packing up the equipment.

"I don't know exactly where you two dragged him to, but if it happens again, I'll sign him into a hospital for rest against his will and put the police on both of you."

Ellen had removed her mask, covered her blonde curls with the wig, and changed clothes just before the doctor arrived. When he left, Powell's maid shooed them out. The actor waved at them with a smile on his face as they left.

The two women entered Powell's office, and went over it again.

"Those shots all went into Councilman Victor, Winnie. None of them came close to Mr. Powell."

"Are you going yell at me anyway for allowing Bill into a dangerous situation?"

"Not a chance. Mr. Powell makes his own decisions and sticks by them. He's a good egg, especially in this town."

"If you want to wrap this up, I recognized the one in the back seat after the window shattered."

"What are we waiting for?"

"We just need to ask Bill a question before we go Sandra."

That evening, the Domino Lady met Scotty and Weed at a hole-in-the-wall bar that still looked like a speakeasy. Sandra was sitting with a male friend two booths away. She flat refused to introduce him to the masked blonde.

"You're not driving off with this one Winnie." The Domino Lady just grinned at her and didn't push it.

Scotty and Weed were full of information, including why Scotty had a broken nose when they met.

"It took Victor two tries to break my nose, and I just had to stand there and take it because we didn't get the ring back."

"Are you trying to get me to feel sorry for you for killing Reuben Victor?"

"Naw, I'm trying to tell you why Weed and I volunteered when Marvin said to get rid of him."

"You're lucky a friend of mine isn't here to turn you over to the cops. Myself, I'm far enough outside the law to know you did everyone a favor, including Reuben Victor."

"How so?" Scotty asked, puzzled at the comment.

"If you and Weed hadn't finished him that quick, Agnes' brother would still be working on him."

Weed shook his head. "No, Mister Green himself told us to make it quick, professional even."

"That seems odd."

Weed spread his hands. "We asked him, but he only said that he got a phone call from a friend who told him it wasn't you, and the only thing he wanted in return was to punch Victor's ticket like it was business and not personal."

"That's all well and good boys, but I needed him to tell the cops I didn't do it."

"Don't worry about that Miss Domino." Weed said. "Mr. Green told us his friend was letting the cops know it was Reuben Victor."

The Domino Lady wrinkled her brow at that, but still pointed toward the door with her chin. "This is the only break you get from me, so try not to cross my path again."

The two mismatched goons quickly picked up their feet and ran for the door. The blonde avenger signaled Sandra to let them go.

"I should probably have shot them both; just a little."

EPILOGUE

*T*wo weeks later, the Domino Lady was back at Powell's home, sipping a martini and enjoying the company.

"So is the ring in a nice, safe place?"

"It is Bill, but I'm still not sure why you want me to keep it for you."

"No one knows who you are, and if people still think I have it, they will keep coming until they get it. I'd rather know it's safe than have someone take it from me again."

"They can still come after you."

Powell shook his head. "I put the word out to a few studio people I know that the ring reappeared, but I handed it over to you so Jean's stepfather couldn't get his hands on it." Powell sighed and shook his head. "Unfortunately, there's some truth behind that statement."

"Was it really that bad?"

"Mama Jean liked to spend her daughter's money, but she never put Jean in a bad situation. That schmuck she married looked at Jean like she was a safety deposit box that never ran out."

"You didn't do anything?"

"There was nothing to do my dear Domino. If I warned him off, Mama Jean would just go into hysterics in front of Jean and she would fold like a set of clean sheets." Powell shook his head.

"I'll give him this, when Jean died, he really was heartbroken."

"Have you heard from Sandra lately?" The Domino Lady changed the subject when she saw Powell suddenly smile. *Probably a memory of Jean.*

"I spoke to her a week ago. She brought in her bill for services and then gave me a big discount." Powell laughed. "She said that she didn't feel right charging me her normal rate since you did so much of the work."

The blonde avenger laughed and handed the actor her glass. "Pour me another one Bill and we'll toast her and that beautiful coupe of hers. Then you can tell me more about Jean"

"Sounds good to me Miss Domino."

"Thank you for coming over tonight Catherine. I trust Anson is well?"

"Yes Douglas. His sons have stayed out of trouble for some time now, they're almost friendly to me even."

"I imagine that will change after his death."

Catherine straightened immediately.

"Is that what this is? A face-to-face order to ...?"

"No! No, Catherine. I simply mean that you shouldn't trust them."

"There's no need to worry about that."

"Good, there are no plans for Anson. Your current life is still secure."

It was a test! Catherine realized. *He just wanted to see how I reacted!*

Douglas told her about the recent events with Ellen Patrick. Once again, the young woman was in the middle of his business, even if she did not realize it.

"You were confident that Ellen wasn't a threat Catherine. She was satisfied with Kynette as the final villain."

"I never said that Douglas. I directed her toward Kynette like you wanted. She seemed happy with that."

"This indicates that you should have done a better job convincing her."

Catherine knew it would do no good to argue, so she changed her tack.

"This only happened because Wilcox is trying to impress you. If he hadn't dragged Edwin in for no real reason, he wouldn't have had a reason to speak to Ellen."

Douglas nodded, smiled, and gave her a short, quick clap.

"Point taken Catherine."

"So what happens to Edwin and Ellen?"

"He's still useful for now. Ellen seems to trust him, so we'll use him to try and get more information out of her. Of course, when he is no longer useful, we'll have Natalie deal with him as you will with Anson eventually." Douglas paused. "Since Ellen apparently has a connection to the Domino Lady, we might even use Edwin to send false information and see what she does with it."

"After Anson met her, before Owen's death, he thought she was too smart and overeducated to become another aging debutante, looking for a husband." Catherine looked at Douglas over her drink. "I think he underestimated her; you should not."

Douglas looked at her like a snake about to eat a rabbit.

"It's odd Catherine. At one moment, you seem to be concerned for Ellen and the next, you seem to want to eliminate her yourself." He smiled slightly and turned his face from her. "I haven't figured out why yet, but I will." He waved at her. "You can go now."

The End

A Domino Lady
Hat Trick

The title means this is my third story, so get your mind out of the gutter. You'll crowd out William Powell thinking about Ellen's .22.

The idea for this tale started with a picture. Specifically, the one which graces the cover of Platinum Girl; a biography of Jean Harlow by Eve Golden. I found it while looking for information on actors and other interesting folks from the 1930s. It struck me how much the pose looked like several covers of on the various Domino Lady comic books and that Harlow could have played an outstanding Ellen Patrick and her masked alter-ego. Hey, the Shadow had a couple of movies by this time, so why not the Domino Lady?

The missing jewelry was originally a ruby necklace, but after I read the biography, I learned about Jean's sapphire ring and how it went missing after her death. As far as anyone knows, the ring was never recovered. Never one to look an historical gift horse in the mouth, I quickly changed the McGuffin to the ring and that brought William Powell into the story as not only a character, but Domino's temporary partner also.

Nearly everyone knows Powell from the Thin Man movies, but he started twenty years earlier playing Vaudeville, and was an established stage actor well before the films. The radiation treatments in the story are real, and were a new, controversial cancer treatment back in the 30s. 'Nicky' beat the odds and lived nearly another fifty years.

I hope fans of Jean Harlow look on this effort with a smile. The more I learned about this original Blonde Bombshell, the more I missed her. She was just beginning to shine as an actress and might have had a career comparable to Barbara Stanwyck or even Lauren Bacall. RIP Jean.

KEVIN FINDLEY - was raised by a kindly couple in a small town in Kansas. Unfortunately, he misplaced his blue suit and red cape as a child, so he has been a freelance writer for the last three years. For three years before that, he edited websites for a number of commercial businesses.

Prior to that, he served 20 years in the U.S. Air Force; retiring as a Logistics Specialist with the rank of Major back in 2009. During that time, he was able to travel and live in various places to include Honduras, Japan, Germany and many more. Surprisingly, he is still allowed in all of those countries. He is married with two kids still at home and more scattered throughout the U.S.

Kevin has been writing in the wonderful worlds of Pulp for just over a year now. You can find him here at Airship 27 in Domino Lady Volume One, The Purple Scar Volume Two and the Tommy Hancock Charity Anthology as well as various publications over at Pro Se Publications. Rumor has it he's working on a historical novel set in ancient Syria.

His wife is very happy he finally listened to her and took up writing as something other than a hobby. It keeps him home, makes a few bucks and keeps him out of trouble for the most part. For more information on what he's doing or just to let him know how much you enjoyed his take on the Masked Rider, you can contact him at www.linkedin.com/pub/kevin-findley/35/208/36a/.

THE DOMINO LADY DECEIVED

By Samantha Lienhard

A young woman stood waiting at the train station, where the luxury train known as the *Flying Eagle* would soon depart for its seaside getaway. Her blonde curls hung immaculately around her face, and she held her suitcase in one delicate, pink-nailed hand.

"Why, if it isn't Ellen Patrick!"

At the sound of the voice, Ellen turned and let out a cry of delight. "Roge, what brings you here today?"

Private investigator Roge McKane crossed the station to reach her, a smile crossing his handsome features as he beheld the young woman who had been his longtime friend. "I'm here to board a train, of course, but I never expected to see you. Are you attending Annabelle Lindh's gala, then?"

With a light, melodious laugh, Ellen shook her head. "Oh no, I've had enough of parties for now. I'm on my way to the coast for a vacation."

The relaxing getaway promised an entire week of sunny weather and peaceful waters.

Roge gave her a wistful smile. "I almost wish I could go with you."

"Oh, would you?" Ellen asked. "I'll be ever so lonely on my own."

Amusement danced in his dark eyes. "Ellen, it will be five minutes before you have charmed every man on the beach."

She wagged her finger at him with a teasing smile. "Not this time, Roge. This week is meant for relaxation, not charming anyone."

"Your charm is not so easily turned off."

Ellen laughed, and in the back of her mind, momentarily wished she was so carefree she truly could get on a train for vacation without any other thought in mind. She had not known that particular brand of freedom since her brief tour of the Far East.

An assassin's bullet had ended that trip, cutting down her father at the command of the state's corrupt political machine. Since then, she had discovered a different sort of freedom, one worlds away from the life she'd grown up expecting to live. With her father's fighting spirit awakened within her, she had devoted herself to seeking vengeance against his enemies, justice for the less-fortunate, and adventure of the finest sort.

"Does this mean you're going to Annabelle Lindh's gala?" she asked, returning to the matter at hand. "I didn't think you were the type."

Roge let out a hearty laugh. "Believe me, I'm not going for the social life. No, me and the boys have been hired by Miss Lindh. As nice as your beachside paradise sounds, I can't skip out on this job now."

"Does she think someone will steal the Star Diamond?" Ellen asked, allowing her eyes to widen slightly as if in shock.

Guards and security made sense for the transport of such a rare and valuable jewel. The prominent debutante Annabelle Lindh had recently come into ownership of the Star Diamond, a diamond that was flawless save for a tiny star-shaped mark at its very center, an unusual feature that made it more valuable than if it had no flaws at all.

Bringing in a private investigator, however, was a step up from normal security.

"With good reason," Roge said. "She didn't want it to go public, but she received a warning from the Domino Lady. The way I hear it, there are rumors that the diamond doesn't rightfully belong to the Lindh family."

Despite feigning ignorance for Roge, Ellen knew exactly what the message said. White ink written on a black card informed Annabelle Lindh that the Star Diamond had once been in the possession of a man named Jirair Sarafian, until he was murdered by someone who fancied the jewel for himself. A bloody trail led the diamond from one owner to the next, until it finally landed in the hands of the Lindh family.

The warning Annabelle Lindh had received encouraged her to bring the Star Diamond's bloody history to light and do what good she could, or the Domino Lady would pay a visit to handle the matter herself.

"But does she really think the Domino Lady will try to take it from the gala?" Ellen asked with a soft laugh. "That might be too dangerous even for her."

"You know as well as I do that she's done the impossible before," Roge said. "But aside from that, it's not just the warning that has Annabelle Lindh on edge."

Ellen looked up sharply. "What do you mean?"

"As I understand it, she's received numerous offers to buy the diamond, with one English gentleman being particularly persistent."

"Goodness, don't tell me she thinks he'll try to steal it."

"Himself? No, she thinks he'll hire someone. She even suggested he put the Domino Lady up to this." Roge laughed again. "Not that I can see the Domino Lady working for someone like that, but who am I to question my employer? Anyway, that's how I'm here waiting for the *Blue Venus.*"

Ellen offered him a warm smile. "I'm sure you'll do wonderfully."

"Thanks, Ellen. There's still time for you to change trains and come with me to the gala."

"And distract you from your work?" she asked. "I wouldn't dream of it. Besides, I'm taking this vacation to relax. Going to a gala, even in such good company, is the opposite of what I have in mind."

The engineer called for everyone to board the *Flying Eagle*, and Ellen lifted her head.

"Goodbye, Roge. You'll have to tell me all about it once you return!"

"I will. You have a good vacation now, you hear?" The private investigator's gaze followed Ellen wistfully as she walked to the train, but he made no move to join her, intent on his own duty regardless of his desires.

Ellen boarded the train and walked to her private cabin, which had been furnished with all the luxuries befitting a passenger of her status.

"Is there anything you need?" the porter asked.

"I'd just like to get some rest," she said, meeting his gaze with a demure smile.

He flushed and looked away from her large brown eyes. "I'll make sure you aren't disturbed."

"Thank you."

The porter closed the door behind him as he left, and Ellen closed her eyes to indeed enjoy a few moments of rest. The train began to move, and soon they were racing down the tracks toward the coast.

Back at the station, Roge would be boarding Annabelle Lindh's private train, the *Blue Venus,* to travel across the state for her gala. He would be on board, as would the young woman and her retinue, and of course, the fabled Star Diamond.

The Star Diamond was indeed a precious jewel, and anyone who owned it would be proud. Ellen didn't know if Annabelle Lindh was complicit in the Star Diamond's bloody history or simply a benefactor of it. Only a few pieces of gossip had met her ears, and the rumors of blackmail and murder could not be definitively tied to the Lindh family.

Yet her reaction to the Domino Lady's warning suggested she at least did not care about the methods used to obtain the Star Diamond, even if she hadn't ordered it herself.

The jewel was out of reach of its rightful owner forever, but that was no reason to reward the callousness through which it had been claimed by allowing it to remain in bloodstained hands. It could be put toward better causes.

Ellen stretched and checked her Baguette watch. She had a few more minutes before she would need to act. For although their destinations were separate, there was a brief window of time when the two trains would run parallel to one another. To most people, that would have meant nothing, even if they knew about the Star Diamond's dark history. But Ellen Patrick was not like most people.

She was the Domino Lady, and the Domino Lady had a job to do.

Ellen slid open the door to her cabin and peered out. The train car was empty for the moment. This would be the most difficult part, when she could not afford to get caught.

She was no longer dressed in the blue dress she wore when Roge saw her onto the train. Now she crept through the silent train dressed in a backless gown of white satin that clung to her curves. A black silk cape covered her shoulders, and a black domino mask obscured the upper part of her face.

For although she was a passenger on the *Flying Eagle*, thus securing her alibi, she intended to steal the Star Diamond—yes, from a train she had never boarded at all!

Ellen took one final look around and then ran to the door, where she stepped out into the fresh air. With a nimbleness that would have shocked anyone who knew her, she crept around the side of the train and clung to it with white-gloved fingers, cape fluttering out behind her as the wind whipped through her hair.

Despite the danger, a thrill coursed through her as the train thundered down the tracks. Ellen took on the role of the Domino Lady for the sake of vengeance, for friendship, and for fighting corruption, but also for the love of adventure itself.

The rumbling of the metal increased, and she lifted her head. Up ahead, the two sets of tracks ran parallel. The *Blue Venus* was coming.

Ellen flattened herself against the side of the train, lest a curious passenger traveling with Annabelle Lindh look out their window and see the Domino Lady poised to leap. She took a breath and gathered her nerve. Never before had she attempted such a daring move; not even the time she was forced to climb across window ledges high above the street did she feel such danger.

At the rate the private train was closing in, she would need to jump in ten more seconds, with perfect timing.

She adjusted her grip on the metal and braced her feet against the side of the train. Eight seconds remained. The two trains were almost on top of each other. Seven. She only had a limited time for the entire operation. The audacity of what she intended threatened to overwhelm her.

Five seconds. A misstep could kill her. If she fell onto the tracks, she risked being stranded at best, crushed at worst. Three seconds. The closest train car had nearly reached her. Two seconds. One.

She leaped!

For a terrifying and exhilarating moment, the young adventuress hung suspended in the air between the two trains, her slender frame at risk of hitting the tracks and being crushed.

Then she landed.

Despite the jolt of impact, she kept enough presence of mind to quickly grab onto the side of the train. Her heart raced from the excitement and danger, and her trembling arms ached for a rest. However, this plan would not allow for such luxuries. The two trains would only run parallel for approximately twenty minutes.

Careful not to pass in front of the windows, Ellen climbed along the side of the train. At last, she circled around to the back of the car and finally allowed herself a moment to recover. Twenty minutes seemed like a fair amount of time—but in that span, she would need to infiltrate the train, locate the Star Diamond, steal it, and get back outside in time to cross back over to her own train.

She peered into the car. It appeared to be a normal passenger car, although a luxurious one, no doubt intended for Annabelle Lindh and her guests. The Star Diamond would be housed somewhere more securely.

With that in mind, Ellen hoisted herself up onto the top of the train. The train's speed as it surged down the track brought her heart into her throat. But she had not earned her reputation as the Domino Lady without possessing strong nerves, and she had a deadline to keep.

Balanced on top of the train car, she dashed to the end. Another great leap from her shapely legs carried her to the next car, and she caught her breath for only a moment before looking inside.

Car by car, she checked the train, until at last she found one that matched her goal.

Unlike the others, this car had no windows. It was also armored, and guards stood stationed around the outside. On the train car across from it, Ellen ducked down before any of the guards could notice her. Undoubtedly there were more guards inside the car, as well.

She had found her destination, but she needed to find a way inside.

Fortunately, they wouldn't expect a thief to come from the top of the train. The guards were patrolling around the exterior of the car, as well as the cars attached to it, no doubt to make sure no one left them. If she could get the guards to leave the door for just a moment, she should be able to slip inside.

Yet the clock was ticking. Presumably they would change shifts at some point, but she couldn't afford to wait them out.

Careful not to make sudden movements that might attract their attention, Ellen slipped her hand into the interior pocket of her cape. She pulled out a small hypodermic syringe filled with a sedative. With her other hand, she withdrew a cluster of metallic beads and cast them down the side of the train car.

Exchanging glances, the two guards started forward, one on each side.

As soon as the closest guard drew near, Ellen dropped down silently from the top of the car. She plunged the hypodermic needle into his neck. He was unconscious before he had time to cry out. Without a pause, Ellen ran past him, a second syringe in hand.

"What—"

She reached the guard just in time to silence him. As he fell, she hurried to the door.

Locked, as expected.

A quick glance at her watch told her she had fifteen minutes left. She crouched alongside the guards and searched them until she found the key to the train car. With a quick glance over her shoulder to make sure no other guards had come by yet, she unlocked the door and opened it a crack.

The interior of the armored car didn't house normal train cabins, but a single chamber with guards patrolling. Ellen waited until the nearest pair of guards had passed, then slipped inside. She crouched in the shadows and waited, aware of the time ticking down.

Two rounds of the guards' patrols was enough to show her she didn't have enough time. She reached into the pocket of her cape again and withdrew a tiny silver sphere filled with a gas that, although harmless, would render anyone who breathed in its fumes unconscious for several minutes. She lobbed it forward.

As soon as the ball struck the floor, it shattered. The startled guards slumped to the ground as they breathed in the gas.

Ellen withdrew a handkerchief treated with the gas's counteragent and pressed it against her face as she dashed past the unconscious guards to the door. She threw it open, reaching for her gun as she did.

The sole guard on duty inside—not Roge, thank goodness—stared at her in alarm, eyes wide, mouth open. Although a cap partly obscured his features, he looked young. They probably put him on duty inside the room since they assumed no one could reach him. No doubt he'd assumed the same.

Ellen snapped up the snub-nose to point straight at him. "Call for help and I'll put a hole straight through your heart!"

He went pale.

"Turn around," she ordered.

The guard hesitated.

"I said, turn around!"

Whether it was her tone or the gun pointed at him, he gulped and turned to face the wall, hands lifted in the air in a sign of surrender. Ellen walked up behind him, gun still held in one hand but now with one last hypodermic syringe in the other. She pressed the needle into the startled guard's neck and injected him without a pause. The fast-acting tranquilizer would knock him out long enough for her to finish the job.

Almost immediately, he slumped to the floor.

Ellen hurried forward to the glass case that contained the Star Diamond. As described, it was a clear, sparkling jewel just small enough to be held between someone's fingers, with a star-shaped flaw at the center. It was easy to understand why Annabelle Lindh prized it so highly. But it did not rightfully belong to her.

Despite the impending deadline if she was to return to her own train in time, Ellen took a moment to study the case. At last, she spotted it—a small wire at the bottom of the glass, nearly invisible at first glance. No doubt it would trigger an alarm.

The young adventuress had much experience disarming such traps, so she swiftly went to work. Finding the edge of the wire, she gripped it between her gloved fingertips and gently guided it out from the binding that attached it to the case, with the most minute of motions to avoid activating it.

It came free, and she breathed a sigh of relief. There were no other traps should could see.

Breath held in anticipation, Ellen lifted the glass case with one hand

and reached in to pick up the Star Diamond with the other. She secured the majestic jewel in the interior pocket of her cape and put a small card under the glass in its place. Written in white ink on black paper, the card read *Compliments of the Domino Lady!*

Then it was time to make her escape.

Leaving the armored car would not be nearly as easy as getting in. By now the guards outside the car would have begun to stir, and she hadn't brought enough gas to use the same trick on them again. Of course, there was the automatic in her hand, but Ellen had yet to take someone's life and didn't intend to cross that line today. Even so, the security on the train was too great for her to fight her way out.

She glanced down at the young man on the floor. He was of medium height and build, only a little taller than her. He had fair hair, too, and as she'd noticed when she confronted him, the way he wore his cap hid part of his face.

An idea took shape in Ellen's mind, though it was insanity to consider such a ploy...

But the Domino Lady had not attained such a notorious reputation by making decisions that were strictly sane.

Facing away from the unconscious and now nearly naked guard to save him further embarrassment, Ellen hiked up the skirt of her gown and slipped her legs into the man's trousers. Both the trousers and his shirt were too large for her, but that helped conceal the bunched up skirt and the cape around her shoulders. As she tucked the last of her blonde curls under the cap, she took a deep breath. This disguise would not hold up under scrutiny, but with the cap angled like he wore it and the too-loose clothes hiding her curves, it should be enough to get her past the guards still disoriented from their unconsciousness.

Ten minutes remained to catch her train.

Ellen gathered her nerve and walked to the door. She slid it open. The guards within the car were still on the ground, though a few had begun to stir. She stepped past them to the outer door. Head slumped, she wrapped her arms around her midriff to both hide how baggy the shirt was on her slender frame and affect an illness.

She opened the door.

The guards outside looked dazed, but their gazes immediately snapped toward her.

"Stomach," she said, pitching her voice into a lower tone. "Must've been something I ate."

"You too, Mitch?" one asked.

"It's not the food," another said. "Something's going on. Some sort of gas."

Ellen offered a short nod and lurched past him as though she was going to be sick.

"Hey—"

She kept walking. If they noticed her shoes, it would be all over. Her skin prickled with the expectation of being chased, but no one followed her. They would check inside the train car first, probably intended to make sure someone took over Mitch's post, and then they'd see what she had done. She quickened her pace.

When she reached the next car, the other guards patrolling barely looked at her. After all, they probably assumed "Mitch" was on break.

The further she got from the armored car, the weaker security became. At last, she crouched outside the door of one car, careful to stay out of view of the windows. She pulled off her cap to let her curls fall free again and returned her domino mask to her face. The borrowed shirt came off next, baring her kissable shoulders to the air as her cape blew out behind her in the fierce wind. She stepped out of the guard's pants and smoothed down her skirt, then braced herself for the exertion to come.

Another bout of climbing brought Ellen to the top of the car, and as she caught her breath, she looked across to the other set of tracks—only to instead see trees and fields where her train should be!

Panic made Ellen gasp, but then she looked further up. The tracks had already begun to diverge, and the car where she had made her ascent was no longer aligned with the parallel section. It wasn't over yet, but she had only a few minutes before she would lose her chance entirely and be stranded on Annabelle Lindh's train where she'd surely be discovered.

She ran.

The wind tossed her curls back as she raced across the top of the train car, speed now taking priority over stealth. She leaped to the next car and kept running despite the impact that jarred her legs. Her shoes were not designed for this sort of activity, and she rarely found herself in situations requiring such a degree of exertion. Yet through all the pain and danger and awareness of her time running out, a thrill coursed through her again.

Up ahead, her train trundled along its tracks, about to turn off.

From the next car, Ellen would be able to make the leap to her destination. She jumped.

In her haste and exhaustion, her timing was off. Her foot slipped, and the young adventuress let out a cry as she lost her balance and tumbled backward over the edge. By instinct, she clutched the top and arrested her fall, but for a moment she dangled there a sickening fear that she wouldn't make it in time.

Ellen pulled herself up with difficulty and balanced on unsteady legs. Across the gap between trains, the *Flying Eagle* was about to make its departure. She gritted her teeth and raced to the edge to make this final jump.

She crashed down onto the top of the *Flying Eagle* just as it rounded the curve of the tracks and left the other train far behind.

Ellen closed her eyes and took a few deep breaths to compose herself. She had made it back. But clinging to the top of a speeding train was not a wise idea, so her return was not quite over yet. After one last moment to steady her nerves and offer her aching muscles respite, she climbed back down the side of the train.

At last, she could take her time again. Best of all, this train didn't have the sort of high security that would lead to someone finding her. No one should have attempted to disturb her while she was "resting" in her private cabin, either.

She made her way through the train slowly and cautiously until she at last returned to the car where this adventure began. Ellen peered inside. One traveler walked through the train car, but soon disappeared into his cabin. She waited another moment to make sure no one else would appear, then slipped in herself.

She opened the door to her cabin. Empty and undisturbed, just as she'd left it, with no sign that anyone had been there. Good. She hurried in and closed the door again.

Just in case anyone would happen to look into the cabin while she was gone, she'd hidden the blue gown she'd been wearing in with her luggage, to make it more likely that they would assume she was simply elsewhere on the train. Ellen opened the suit case and pulled out the blue dress, smoothly out the material before setting it down.

Then she removed her domino mask and slipped out of her cape and white gown. Folded up together with everything else she had taken along for the adventure, including the Star Diamond itself, she hid them at the

She jumped.

very bottom of the suitcase and closed it.

With that taken care of, Ellen at last dressed in the soft blue dress and combed her hair to remove any signs that she had been outside in the wind. A small hand mirror let her examine her appearance, and she made sure she looked like she had indeed been resting in her cabin.

If only it were true. She closed her eyes and let out a long breath. Her entire body ached, and it would surely feel worse before it got better. Nevertheless, she needed to cement her alibi and keep up appearances, so she only stayed in her cabin a few moments longer.

Then she opened the door and headed to the dining car.

Several other passengers were inside already, and they looked up as she entered.

Ellen greeted them with a bright smile. "It's been a lovely ride so far, hasn't it? I hope you won't mind me joining you for dinner."

By evening, the train had arrived at the coast. Ellen entered her luxurious hotel room and lay back on the large bed with a sigh. At last, she could relax. Her aching muscles welcomed the soft bed beneath her. A slight smile curved her lips as she imagined the chaos that must have erupted on Annabelle Lindh's train after her departure. They must be frantically trying to learn how the Domino Lady eluded them. Would they suspect she had left the train, or would they investigate all of the passengers instead?

Poor Roge. She must have caused him a terrible headache, as he would have to deal with this mess, but it was unavoidable that sometimes they were brought into conflict.

The most important thing was that she had secured the Star Diamond. All that remained was getting rid of it. She would have liked to return it to its rightful owner, but the rumors about Jirair Sarafian made no mention of any descendants.

As per her usual habits, then, she would fence the diamond once enough time had passed for it to not be too hot to be put on the market. A fraction of the proceeds would go toward financing her own lifestyle, while the bulk would be donated to charities. Anonymous donations from the Domino Lady had done a great deal of good throughout the state of California, and she could think of no better way to subvert the Star Diamond's bloody history.

Of course, the diamond itself would end up in the hands of someone undeserving, but here their efforts would go toward a good cause.

In the morning, she would mail herself the diamond in a large envelope she had packed with her things for this purpose. Keeping it in her suitcase for the entire vacation was far too risky.

Ellen double-checked to make sure her door was locked and then opened up her suitcase. She got out the envelope first and placed it on the bed, then dug through her clothes to find the bundle she had hidden at the bottom when she returned to the train. It was probably best if she mailed everything to herself, gown and cape and gun as well as the diamond.

She opened the cape's interior pocket and pulled out the jewel. Strange that something so small could cause so much death. The diamond glittered in the light, beautiful and precious.

Yet as the light caught its facets, Ellen frowned. She lifted it to her face to study it more closely.

The Star Diamond's fame came from two things: the tiny star-shaped flaw at its very center, and the otherwise flawless nature of the jewel. But this diamond's star wasn't truly at the center. She turned it over slowly to look at it from all sides. From other angles, and with the luxury of time she didn't have when she took it from Annabelle Lindh's secure train car, it was clear the star was not a flaw in the diamond but one etched onto the outside.

Descriptions of the Star Diamond were clear. If it was a mistake, rumors would have gotten out after all this time. That only left one possibility. Someone had taken a flawless diamond of the same size and shape and disguised it to look like the Star Diamond before placing it in the glass case—*the diamond Ellen had stolen was a fake!*

Since Ellen was officially on vacation and Annabelle Lindh's gala was miles away, there was no way she could return for the true Star Diamond without arousing suspicions. Although fury at being tricked made her anxious to settle this immediately, she also had to consider the possibility that this was an intentional trap. They might have done this not only to protect the Star Diamond, but to provoke her into doing something foolish.

Never had she imagined they would take such extensive precautions. They had set up excessive security around a replica to throw would-be thieves off the track, while transporting the actual Star Diamond elsewhere.

By necessity, this had become a slower game. While Ellen planned for her next opportunity, she would also need to erase any suspicion that might be around herself—she wouldn't underestimate them again—by making her vacation feel real.

So she outwardly put the incident out of her mind and enjoyed the other vacationers on the beach. She relaxed in the sun, stretching her lithe body as though she had not a care in the world. She swam for a time as well, and joined the other guests for dinner that evening. She spoke to them about harmless topics, and although the subject of Annabelle Lindh came up once or twice, she merely listened without asking any questions.

Her original vacation plans had allowed her a week on the beach. Unless she found a good excuse to leave early, she might need to remain there for the entire duration.

Yet she could at least put that time to good use. She needed to plan how she would steal the actual Star Diamond. If Annabelle Lindh put it on display at the gala, that would be a good time to take it, but she wouldn't be able to make it there in time. Besides, there was a chance they would use another fake. No, she would need to pinpoint how and where the true diamond would be stored, and then claim it.

It was also possible the diamond had never been taken to the gala at all and remained securely held at a place such as the Lindh Estate.

These musings occupied Ellen through the night. In the morning, she stretched beneath the soft blankets of her luxurious bed and considered the matter once again. As long as she had enough patience, she would be successful. If they thought she had been deceived by the replica, so much the better. She wouldn't draw attention to the decoy until she was ready to claim the original. Perhaps she would even play their own trick on them and swap the replica back in exchange for the real one. With a soft laugh, she stretched and rose for the day.

Ten minutes later, Ellen wore a summer dress in shades of pink that complemented her painted nails, and sat in the hotel's grand dining area with other guests who trickled in one or two at a time to partake of breakfast ahead of the day's relaxation.

Breakfast came in the form of an omelet and toast. While Ellen ate, she picked up the day's newspaper so she could page through it for both entertainment and potential information.

The headline on the front page made her stop short.

Star Diamond Stolen! Domino Lady Absconds With Precious Jewel!

No longer interested in breakfast, Ellen turned her full attention to the article. It went on to state that despite the security Annabelle Lindh had on the train, her precious Star Diamond had been stolen during the journey by the Domino Lady. A solid recounting of events, if somewhat dramatized for the paper, detailed Ellen's confrontation with the guards and how the masked vigilante had seemingly vanished from the train with the Star Diamond in hand.

Both the hired detectives and the police would attempt to track down the Domino Lady. Although she was notoriously difficult to catch, Annabelle Lindh had insisted on it, with a full half a page devoted to the debutante's hysterical quotes about how such a precious treasure needed to be restored to her at any cost.

Ellen slowly set down the newspaper. This called into question everything she'd pieced together since she discovered the replica jewel.

One possibility was that they believed she wouldn't have noticed the deception yet, and this was a show meant to convince her she'd stolen the actual Star Diamond. Yet the replica didn't seem designed to fool a close study, which they had to assume would occur as soon as the Domino Lady tried to fence it.

Another possibility was that Annabelle Lindh had hidden the Star Diamond away in order to gain insurance money by claiming it had been stolen. Since there was little chance the police could get it back, she would be successful. Yet the article went into great detail about her insistence that the diamond be recovered, to the point where it didn't seem like she would be satisfied with an insurance payout.

A third possibility was that she had an associate in need of boosted social standing, perhaps a detective or police officer, who would "recover" the diamond for her and become a hero as a result, but that suggested a sort of generosity yet to be demonstrated by the Lindh family.

"Wild news, isn't it?" One of the men staying at the hotel paused by Ellen's table and nodded toward the paper. "I'd like to meet a dame like that Domino Lady someday. Seems she can get away with just about anything."

Ellen's melodious laugh masked her confusion about what had happened. "To think that someone could steal the Star Diamond out from all that security. It's amazing. Don't the police have any idea how she managed it?"

"Nope. Near as they can figure, she must have jumped from the moving train to make her escape—but that's about as fantastic as her disappearing into thin air!"

"Is it possible this is actually some sort of publicity stunt," Ellen asked, choosing her words with care, "and the diamond hasn't truly been stolen at all?"

A woman at the next table looked over. "Haven't you heard? Miss Lindh is furious about the theft! She fired pretty much everyone who was on security that day."

The man laughed. "If it really is a stunt, she's a heck of an actress."

"I can't blame her for being upset," the woman said. "Do you have any idea of how much she built her image on being the owner of the Star Diamond? Without that, what is she? Losing it in such a way will damage her reputation even further as well."

As the conversation continued, Ellen kept up a polite façade of interest and offered her own comments from time to time.

Inwardly, she reluctantly conceded the point. Annabelle Lindh would lose too much in reputation and social standing from the Star Diamond's theft, which gave her no motive to stage the incident herself.

That left only one final possibility.

She thought the jewel stolen from the train was truly the Star Diamond. She hadn't placed the decoy there at all and had no idea it was a fake.

Someone else had beaten Ellen to it and stolen the Star Diamond first.

That evening, the phone in Ellen's hotel room rang while she was sitting in bed with a cup of tea, trying to work through her next plan of how to track down the thief. She answered it in a soft voice, curious about who might have reached out to her while she was on vacation. "Hello?"

Roge's voice greeted her on the other end. "How's your vacation?"

"It's lovely here," she said, straightening up. "I understand you've had your fair share of excitement, though."

"Tell me about it," he said. "It's been crazy."

"Did the Domino Lady really steal the Star Diamond from a moving train?"

"She did. Everything seemed fine at first. The train car was secured, plenty of guards all around it. I checked all the passengers to make sure everyone was who they were supposed to be. It was mainly Miss Lindh's social circle, after all. Everyone checked out."

"Then is one of them the Domino Lady?" she asked, curious about what Roge's reasoning would be in regard to how the theft played out.

"Hard to say. No way an imposter slipped through on the passenger list, though. So partway through the journey, there was a commotion. The guards around the train car were knocked out, and we found the guard who was in there *with* the diamond knocked out too, and without his clothes on—begging your pardon, Ellen."

She smiled with amusement. "Please, go on."

"He said it was the Domino Lady who did it to him, and sure enough, her calling card was there. Turns out the guards outside thought he had gone past them a little while earlier. It seems she disguised herself as the unfortunate man and walked straight out past the guards. Well, we found his clothes discarded in one of the train cars, but then we checked all the passengers again and no one had the Star Diamond. We combed over the entire train."

"How is that possible?" Ellen asked.

"The running theory is that she jumped from the moving train, but... that's daring, even for her. Some of the boys think she was one of the passengers after all and just found a way to ditch the diamond before we got to her."

"That sounds so dangerous, even for the Domino Lady," Ellen said, letting a note of awe and fear enter her voice. "Would she truly risk her life just to steal a jewel? Isn't it possible she stole the Star Diamond before the train left the station?"

Roge chuckled. "I thought about that too. If that happened, she could've been one of the passengers and just staged the commotion to make people think the diamond was safe until then. But it was in the custody of Miss Lindh's guards and they all swear up and down the Star Diamond was on board the train when we left."

"Oh my, that's what I get for trying to help," Ellen said with laughter of her own. "I have no head for this sort of detective work."

"Don't be ridiculous, Ellen. Where would I be if I couldn't talk over my cases with you?"

This time she made herself sound hesitant, not entirely feigned since she didn't want to draw attention to her line of questioning. "Could she have had help?"

"Maybe so," Roge said. "Remember what I said about those buyers?"

That was right; he had said something about people offering to buy the Star Diamond from Annabelle Lindh, to the point where she had become concerned that they might be working with the Domino Lady. "You mentioned an English gentleman..."

"That's right, calls himself Lord William Langdale, though it's not clear if he's really nobility or if he just likes to style himself 'Lord.' I figured it was just paranoia to think he might have been working with the Domino Lady, but he's rich enough to finance a major operation. Could have given her some help."

Interesting. Ellen took another sip of her tea. Perhaps this Englishman was the one who had beaten her to the chase. She would need to learn who he was and see how she might best approach the matter of locating the Star Diamond.

"I'm still on the case," Roge said. "Miss Lindh is insistent that we get her diamond back. I've got half a hope the Domino Lady might turn the diamond over to the police like she sometimes does, but there's no sign of that happening."

It certainly wouldn't happen, even if she found the diamond again. The police would see Annabelle Lindh as its rightful owner, and it did not belong to her.

But what was this Lord William's claim to the Star Diamond?

"Now, enough about me," Roge said. "Tell me more about your vacation. I sure wish I could be there."

Ellen spent the rest of the conversation telling her old friend about the beach and the hotel, with her interest in learning more about his case disguised behind a polite façade of enjoying her vacation.

"Sounds like you're having a wonderful time," Roge said. "Sorry for talking your ear off about my case while you're trying to rest."

"Think nothing of it, Roge. On the contrary, from the moment I read about the Star Diamond's theft, I couldn't wait to talk to you and find out what happened."

"I just hope I won't have to go up against the Domino Lady. After everything she's done, I admit I sympathize with her more often than not." He sighed. "Anyway, I'm sure you have things to do. Enjoy your vacation, Ellen."

"Thank you. I'm sure everything will work out."

Ellen hung up the phone and finished her tea as she thought everything over. The conversation with Roge had provided more questions than answers, but those questions also included a wealth of information that could put her on the right track.

First, the swap happened before the Star Diamond was placed on the train. Since all of the passengers had been cleared, the only other possibility would be if someone else had gotten on the train and then off again before she did. Unlikely.

Second, if the decoy had been on the train from the start, then at least one of the guards had to be in on the plot.

Third, this Lord William sounded like the most likely culprit, to the point where it had been proposed that he and the Domino Lady were working together. His insistence on buying the diamond must have been enough to cast suspicion on him.

Ellen set her teacup aside and flopped backward onto her pillows. In some ways, the mysterious thief had done her job for her. The Star Diamond was out of Annabelle Lindh's hands. It was tempting to let the police recover the decoy Star Diamond and have them think the entire matter was over and done with, although it probably wouldn't take them long to discover the deception.

More importantly, she had no way of knowing the thief had any more right to the Star Diamond. For all she knew, Lord William's hands were just as bloody.

Until she had her answers, the job wasn't quite over yet.

Gossip was an invaluable source of information. Over the years, Ellen learned she had no need of an intelligence network when casual conversation with the right people could provide her with the little details she needed to piece together the bigger picture.

Everyone was abuzz about the Star Diamond's theft. It hardly took effort to steer any conversation around to the Domino Lady and speculation about how she might have gotten away with such a precious jewel. Most people had at least one theory, some of which got to be quite fantastic. Ellen would have been flattered by what they deemed her capable of if she hadn't known the true thief performed a heist even better than hers and went undetected while she got "credit" for the theft.

If there was one benefit of this, it was that the increased gossip around the Star Diamond had dredged up fragments of its dark history. The bloody trail that brought the diamond into Annabelle Lindh's hands had been dragged into the light as everyone searched for the stolen jewel. Yet the debutante herself remained undeterred. With rumors about the diamond's ownership swirling around the social circles, she had rescheduled her gala until the Star Diamond could be recovered and doubled down on her insistence that the diamond must be returned to her.

It also didn't take much work to learn more about Ellen's top suspect. A few casual questions about Lord William Langdale revealed a mountain of gossip surrounding his love of art and his dubious claim of being nobility—a claim which, people whispered, came more from his great wealth than any actual family status.

There were, in fact, many rumors about him. This wasn't the first time his spotless reputation had been called into question, but any questions about him always disappeared into nothing... a trick likely enabled by the large amounts of money he could use to buy most people's silence.

Overall, while there was nothing definitive, he had the potential to be as corrupt as any of the people the Domino Lady had targeted in the past.

And while balmy afternoons at the beach and lighthearted dinners in the hotel provided gossip for Ellen to sift through, conversations with Roge revealed new details about the investigation itself.

Security on the train had been boosted due to the threats against the Star Diamond, which meant some of the guards on the train were new. One of them had previously been employed by none other than Lord William, but despite the rumors that fueled, Roge had abandoned it as a lead since the guard had an alibi for the period of time when the Domino Lady was on the train.

If only he knew the actual diamond had been stolen earlier, perhaps they could have found a clue, but there was no way she could safely let Roge in on that information. They were unable to trace anything back to Lord William himself either.

Newspapers began to run stories about how he had wanted the Star Diamond, but those stories quickly disappeared in favor of more sensational articles about the Domino Lady. Anything leading back to him vanished to leave behind only dead ends.

And so, when Ellen's week-long vacation came to an end, she postponed her return home and let her friends know she intended to do a little more vacationing after all and take a trip to refresh herself—a trip to England.

The Langdale Estate was located at the top of a cliff overseeing the ocean. In sharp contrast to the sunny shores Ellen had left, here violent waves crashed against the rocks as storm clouds gathered overhead. For the past week, she had taken nightly trips to the cliff to observe the estate, until at last she was ready to make her move.

There were, in fact, many rumors about him.

Her black cape partly shielded her from the spray of ocean water that otherwise pierced the thin silk of her white gown as she crept toward the base of the cliff. Although it must have been chosen for its natural defenses, years of wind and rain and ocean spray had eroded paths and ledges into the rocky face. After Ellen's race across the train cars, such a trek almost sounded relaxing for the young adventuress.

How people who knew Ellen Patrick would stare if they could see her creeping through the night up the side of a mountain, her face hidden by a domino mask, prepared to risk life and limb in pursuit of the truth.

Her nightly surveillance had shown her that the guards followed strict patrols. Time was on her side this time, so she would preferably have no need for the direct confrontations she'd used on the train. Six sets of guards patrolled in each shift, each set a pair of armed men who guard a particular section of the estate's grounds. Sometimes they crossed paths and switched areas, perhaps to avoid the dangers of corruption by ensuring the same guard wouldn't be guarding the same spot all night long. However, there was a pattern to these movements as well, and Ellen had watched them long enough to learn their routine.

Slipping past the patrols would take impeccable timing. The challenge sent a thrill through her as she imagined the task again.

The rough path worn into the side of the cliff brought Ellen around to the back of the estate. Back there, neatly trimmed grass gave way only to hedges landscaped in the shape of wild animals. They were like works of art themselves, great guardians that looked over the estate. She crouched down in the shadows of a tiger and waited.

One pair of guards passed. A rasher vigilante might have darted forward immediately, but patience was often the key to victory. Ellen waited.

The same pair returned on their second patrol. Still, she waited. Without knowing which part of the routine she'd arrived at, any sudden move could put herself unnecessarily at risk.

They made a third pass, but then they turned. Yes, that meant it was time for them to switch. Another pair of guards walked forward from the adjacent section of the grounds and took up their patrol instead.

Based on the pattern she'd learned during her observations, the patrols would make somewhere between five and seven passes before they would switch with the next set of guards. She hadn't determined if there was also a pattern to as to which number they chose, but it didn't matter for her mission. Be it five passes or seven, this gave her the window she needed to get past them.

The new pair of guards passed by on their patrol. Once they were out of sight, Ellen dashed forward.

She crossed the yard and pressed herself flat against the estate wall. As the guards continued patrolling, she crept through the shadows. Whenever a patrol passed, she ducked behind cover. In this way, she slowly made her way to a small door.

From her observations, aided by binoculars, at least one servant usually left via this exit in the evenings.

Sure enough, after a few minutes of waiting, the door opened. A young woman stepped out and walked forward to be cleared by security before leaving the grounds. As the guards spoke to her, Ellen slipped in through the door before it closed.

Inside, she found herself in a small hallway, possibly part of the mansion used by the servants to get around. Since she had never gone inside the estate before, she would be traveling blind from here on in.

Footsteps and voices echoed from down the hallway. Ellen froze and looked around for some means of escape. Her gaze landed on a small door to her right. She opened it onto what was fortunately an empty room and darted inside. Then she crouched down and listened.

The voices got closer and closer, and then continued past.

She exhaled and opened the door again. The hallway was clear. Alert for any sign of danger, she crept through the manor's long hall. At the corner, she turned and continued her search, with the manor relatively free of activity due to the time of night.

At last, she reached a set of double doors. Elaborate designs carved into the thick wood suggested they barred the way to something important. Her heart leaped. This might be what she was looking for. The halls remained empty for the moment, so she listened at the door. Silence. She carefully opened the door a crack. No one was inside. It appeared to be an art gallery of some sort.

Ellen slipped inside and gasped in spite of the need for stealth. The room was massive, with a marble floor and a high domed ceiling that gave it the strange sense of being a cathedral. Sculptures and works of art on plinths filled the room in orderly rows, and paintings hung along all the walls. This left no room for windows, but light entered the room instead from a massive skylight in the shape of a rose, through which the moon shone down upon the crown jewel of the gallery: the Star Diamond.

She cautiously walked through the gallery. Some of the art on display was unfamiliar to her, but others she recognized as having been auctioned off to a mystery buyer. Then there were a few she had seen other places on display—unless they were duplicates themselves, apparently the Star Diamond wasn't the only thing Lord William had stolen and replaced with a replica.

No wonder he coveted the Star Diamond. If these were his tastes, such a rare and beautiful jewel fit his collection perfectly.

It sat beneath a glass case, much as it had on the train, although the security around it was less apparent. Did Lord William trust his servants and staff so much he didn't bother to hide or even *protect* his stolen goods?

Ellen stepped around the diamond's plinth to view it from all sides. Its facets glimmered in the moonlight. Yes, this truly was the Star Diamond. The star-shaped flaw was within the stone, not etched on the outside like on the copy.

With a quiet *snk*, the gallery doors opened.

Her heart leaped into her throat, and she ducked out of sight behind a large sculpture of a woman standing by a tree. She held her breath.

The man who entered the gallery wasn't Lord William, but he didn't look like security. He was small in stature, with dark hair swept back from his gaze. He wore loose-fitting black clothes and made no sound as he walked across the marble floor of the gallery. His movements were precise, practiced—the walk of a thief?

His gaze scanned the gallery. He continued walking forward.

Ellen reached for her automatic and wrapped her fingers around it. So far, he hadn't seen her. If it looked like he wasn't going to leave, she could use the advantage of surprise to get away.

Halfway through the room, he stopped. "I know you're in here, Domino Lady."

She went completely still.

"Let's be reasonable about this." His voice was soft, but there was an unpleasant edge of humor in it, as if he was taunting her for being discovered even though he had yet to look at her. "We aren't your enemies. Lord William only wants to talk to you."

Ellen scanned the room. There were no windows save for the ceiling skylight, so she would have to use the door. Escape was still possible. Although he spoke with complete confidence that she was in there, he addressed the gallery as a whole, suggesting he didn't know her precise location. If she used the art displays as her cover, she could make her way to the exit. While her pursuer searched for her in the gallery, she could sneak behind him and back out into the hallway—although if he'd brought guards with him, her escape might be short-lived.

"No response?" he asked. "Perhaps you're hoping I'll assume you aren't here at all and I'm speaking to an empty room."

That would be helpful. No one had seen her approach the estate, and she'd employed stealth once she entered the manor. Ellen saw no possible way this man *could* genuinely know she was in the gallery. He was bluffing, hoping the audacity of addressing her directly would lure her out of hiding.

He didn't appear at all bothered by the possibility that he was alone. "Perhaps you aren't here at all, Domino Lady, or perhaps you are only hoping to make me believe as much. It doesn't matter. I am a patient man."

So he would either search the room or wait her out. Hiding there wouldn't be an option forever. She needed to escape.

"Is this the game we're playing?" As he spoke, his gaze wandered toward one of the large sculptures on the other side of the room. He strolled behind it and around the other side, his gait as casual as if he were merely enjoying the scenery rather than searching. "Or are you simply too frightened to move?"

He strolled toward another one of the plinths, and Ellen braced herself. Once he turned to look behind it, his back would be to her. She could slip to the next display.

"Then again..." He paused and turned to inspect the sculpture that had caught his eye.

Ellen moved, as silent as possible.

"...you could be planning your escape." The man whirled around mid-step just as Ellen emerged from behind cover.

Her heart leaped into her throat, but it was too late. With a smirk, he raced toward her, and she dashed for the door. His path veered and he cut her off even as she stumbled backward to avoid being caught.

She snapped up her gun and aimed the snub-nosed automatic straight at him. "Get out of my way. Make a sound and they'll be seeing daylight through you!"

He had the audacity to laugh. "You're not going to shoot me."

Ellen narrowed her eyes behind her mask and released the safety on the gun.

The man didn't even flinch. "For one thing, the sound of a gunshot will also bring Lord William's security running. That will be ten, possibly even twenty armed guards. Can you fight so many at once? And unless you take me out immediately, I'll have enough time to cry for help and tell them exactly where to go."

"You won't live that long," she said, her voice cold.

Still, he only smiled. Overconfidence? Or was it something deeper?

At the current range, she *would* kill him immediately if she fired. Practice had taught her as much. But...

"But more importantly," he said, almost as though he had read her thoughts, "I've heard it said the Domino Lady has never killed anyone. Is today truly the day you want to cross that line?"

Not at all. The thought of becoming a murderer filled her with dread and guilt. Yet if it came down to a choice between the two of them, what would she do? Usually threats were enough to cow an adversary, but that would not work here.

"Since you seem to have ignored me the first time," he said with a weary sigh as though he was a long-suffering host dealing with a troublesome houseguest, "let me tell you again that we are not your enemies."

"You expect me to believe that?" she demanded.

"I could have brought twenty men in here to retrieve you by force," he said, "but Lord William prefers to receive you as an honored guest. In light of that, are you still willing to kill me?"

She lowered her gun and put it away.

Then she bolted for the door.

This time, her sudden movement took him by surprise. He lunged at her, but she stayed just out of his grip. A wild exhilaration filled her, and she threw the gallery doors open.

A dozen armed security guards stood waiting. She froze.

The man strolled after her into a hall. A slow smile spread across his face. "Now, wouldn't you rather discuss this like reasonable people?"

Lord William was a large man, balding, dressed in a crisp white suit, with the sort of imposing presence that came from more than his physical stature alone. Smoke from a thick cigar wreathed around his face as Ellen entered the parlor, escorted by the man who had found her in the gallery.

He'd taken her gun but made no mention of her removing her mask, and he'd treated her almost courteously since her surrender in the hall. Yet she remained tense, alert for anything that might happen. Lord William wanting to speak with her was almost more alarming than if he had tried to unmask her. There was no telling what he might have in mind.

The parlor was small and cozy, with a fireplace crackling beneath a painting of the manor's owner himself and furniture of a high quality that matched the other tastes she had noticed in her time on the estate.

"So at last I meet the infamous Domino Lady." William waved his hand at the plush chair opposite his. "Sit down."

She sat.

The other man walked around to stand alongside William's chair, just behind his right shoulder. In contrast to the humor he displayed in the gallery, he appeared completely impassive.

"Would you like a cigar?" William asked. Then he began chuckling. "Forgive me. With a woman of your reputation, I don't know what to expect."

"No thank you," Ellen said. It was difficult to tell if he meant the offer as praise or insult.

He took one more puff of his own cigar and then set it aside on the small table alongside his chair. "Welcome to my manor." He nodded toward the man who had found her in the art gallery. "I trust Barsegh gave you a warm welcome."

Ellen folded her arms. "Let's just say he made meeting with you an offer I couldn't refuse."

"Did he now? I am pleased with your services, Barsegh, as always."

Barsegh inclined his head. "The pleasure is mine."

"Let me tell you something, Domino Lady," William said, leaning forward, "if you ever have to hire someone, hire a foreigner. They have no ties that could turn them against you."

She glanced up at Barsegh again, but his face remained expressionless, undoubtedly a practiced skill unless it was his liveliness in the gallery that was the façade.

Lord William leaned back in his chair again. "Now, let us get down to business! Do not look so anxious. You are among friends here. You may call me William, and I will call you—" He paused and chuckled. "Forgive me, is there a name you would like me to use?"

As if she would give up her name so easily.

"Domino Lady it is, then. A pity." He shrugged. "No matter, we are still here together. I have wanted to meet you for a long time, Domino Lady. At last, when I learned of the Star Diamond, I knew I had found my opportunity!"

Ellen gave him a sharp look. "You stole the Star Diamond in order to meet *me*?" Of all things, she hadn't expected that.

He let out another hearty laugh. "Oh, adding the Star Diamond to my collection was a chance I couldn't overlook. It makes quite the shining centerpiece of my gallery, don't you think? Poor Annabelle Lindh, running around in such desperation as she tries to find her jewel. I may never be able to quite look her in the eye again, although she never deserved such a precious thing."

He was right about that much, at least.

"But I might have waited a long time before claiming the Star Diamond—certainly until she recovered from her paranoia after my attempts to buy it—until I learned the infamous Domino Lady had sent Annabelle a warning. Then I knew I must act and put Barsegh to work immediately!"

So Barsegh was the one who had actually stolen the diamond and perhaps made a bargain with the guards as well. She'd suspected as much from their encounter in the gallery. He moved with the grace and poise of a thief, and his levelheaded reasoning would serve him well in tense situations.

He met her gaze and this time he almost smiled, a glimmer of the attitude he'd shown during their confrontation.

She returned her gaze to William. "So you had the Star Diamond stolen and replaced with a decoy, knowing I would discover the replica and begin searching for the true jewel. Why? What do you want with me?"

"We are kindred spirits, my dear!" He waved his hand toward the far side of the parlor, where a large cabinet contained bottles and glasses. "If not a cigar, would you like some brandy?"

"No thank you."

"Then what would you like? You are my honored guest, after all."

"I want answers," she said, annoyed by his false camaraderie when he had effectively taken her prisoner. "Why do you think we're alike?"

"We are two free spirits poised against a world that has tried to confine us. I am sure you are a lady of means; no one could pull off such feats without considerable resources, and your heists would have long since funded a comfortable life by now. What could possibly drive such people as you and I to a life of crime? It is the thrill, my dear, a thrill we cannot get anywhere else! The world would have us fit neatly into the molds it has made for us, but we refuse its restrictions."

Ellen watched him through narrowed eyes. How little he knew about her. She had donned the mask of a vigilante in response to her father's death, to fight the corruption that had killed him.

Yet there *was* some truth to William's words. The thrill of danger as she pulled off a perfectly-executed heist or narrowly escaped danger was unmatched by anything else. Ellen Patrick in her normal life would never engage in such adventures, but the Domino Lady had the freedom to do so much more.

As much distaste as she felt for this man who stole things for his own personal collection rather than any good cause, they were not entirely dissimilar.

William cleared his throat. "Barsegh, let us not make the mistake of underestimating the Domino Lady. See to it that the gallery is free from any tricks she might have placed there before you arrived."

With a short bow, Barsegh departed the room.

Then the two of them were alone.

"What is it you want from me?" Ellen asked again.

"Straight to the point, I see. Good! That's the sort of attitude I like to see. No point in bandying about meaningless trivialities, eh?" William gave her an approving nod. "I will also get straight to the point, then: I want to propose a partnership."

She stared at him.

"My arrangement with Barsegh works quite well," he said, "but I could use someone with your talents. There are places even he cannot access that I daresay the Domino Lady could find a way to enter. Besides, our partnership has begun to wear on me as of late. I fear the time is coming when Barsegh and I will part ways."

"You want me to steal things for you?" she asked.

"I don't want you to go out of your way," he said with a shrug. "I merely propose that when you find yourself compelled to remove an item from its current owner, you will have a buyer waiting to take it off your hands and give it a new home."

Meaning his gallery, of course.

"There might be times when I have something particular in mind. In that case, I would humbly request you to turn your attention to it. However, you will largely have freedom to act as you always have, but now you will be well-compensated."

Ellen bristled. He called them kindred spirits, and it seemed he truly believed it—he thought she would steal anything if she was paid for it and give it to him for his collection. His interest in the Star Diamond had intrigued her, but clearly he had no idea that its dark history was what made her target Annabelle Lindh.

"Speechless, are you?" he asked. "Is there something in my proposed terms that has you concerned? Please, make your case. I am a reasonable man."

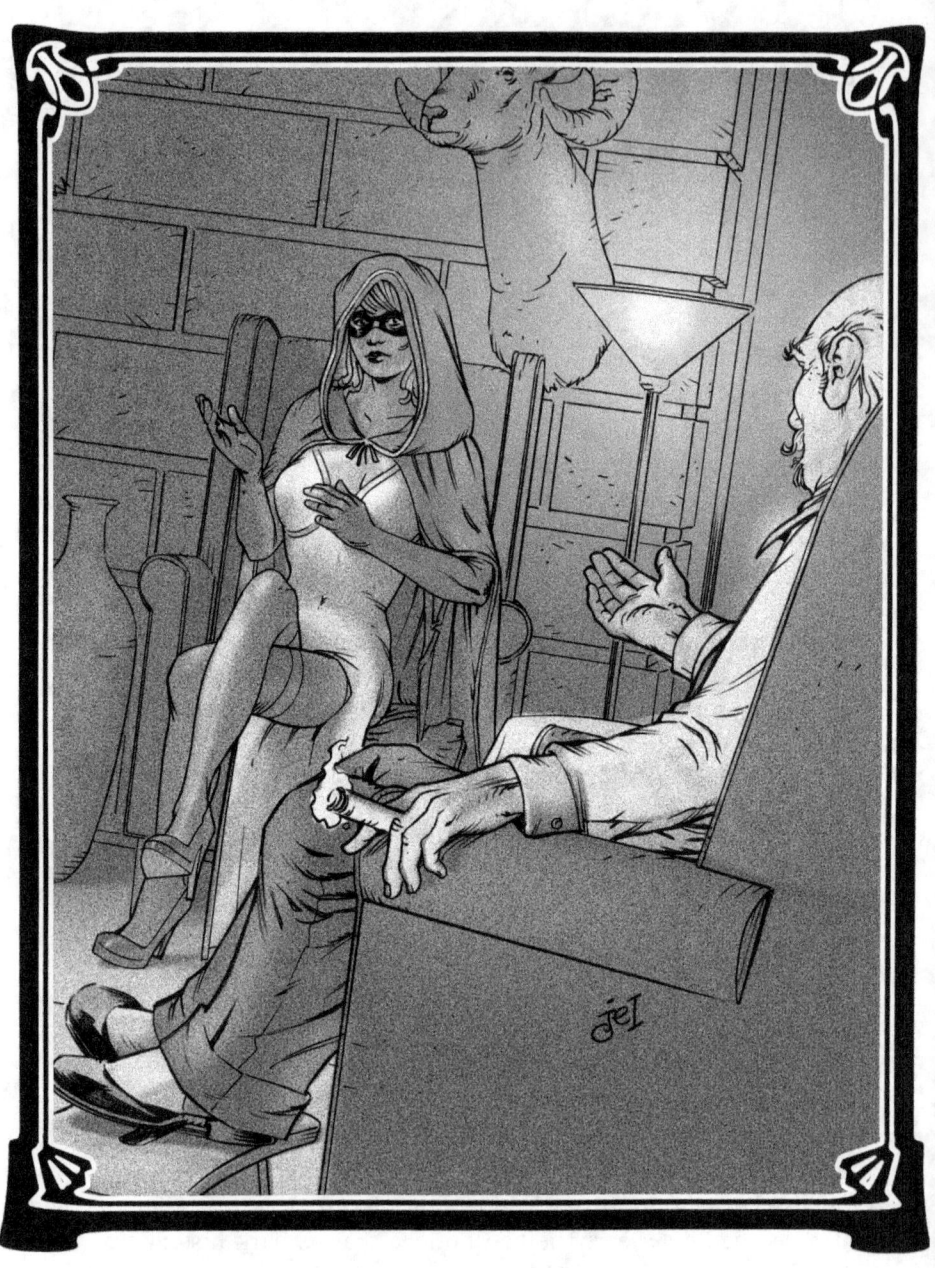

"You want me to steal things for you?"

Ellen folded her arms. "I have a feeling ours would be an even more temporary partnership than your arrangement with Barsegh."

His low, rumbling laugh gave no sign of any dismay he might feel. "Is that so?"

"Yes," she said. "Thank you for the offer, but I must refuse."

William let out a long sigh. "I suppose that is your final answer, then."

"It is."

"Regrettable, but I suppose it's always a gamble when one proposes such a partnership. Very well, Domino Lady, you may leave with my blessing." He waved his hand toward the door. "No one will impede you."

She rose from her seat.

Although William remained sitting, his gaze followed her as she walked to the parlor door. "I should warn you, however, that I sincerely hope you do not harbor any delusions of turning me in for my thefts."

She paused with her hand on the doorknob. Although the thought of turning him in had crossed her mind, she had been much more interested in reclaiming the Star Diamond from him. His threat would be worth hearing out.

"If you act against me," he said, "I will be forced to respond in kind."

Ellen turned to face him, but said nothing. He was a rich and powerful man. He could frame the Domino Lady for crimes she would never commit and seek his vengeance in that way—but she had dealt with such situations before and come out on top.

"Barsegh is quite capable. I've never seen a man so capable of tracking his quarry. If you make yourself my enemy, I will set him on your heels. He will find you and learn who you truly are, and then I will destroy everything you have built."

So that was his game.

"I understand," she said.

He smiled, jovial and affable once again. "Do not think I mean our relationship to end on a sour note, however. Speak to Barsegh on your way out. I have prepared to pay you a sizable amount for the Star Diamond. It should make up for leaving you with a replica."

Once again, he assumed profit was her only reason for going after the Star Diamond. He did not deserve it any more than Lady Annabelle did.

Ellen turned and strode out of the parlor.

The following night, she returned, clad once again in her mask and cape.

More alert than ever, she crept up the path worn into the cliff. Since Lord William had predicted she would track the Star Diamond to him, he might also predict she would come back. Then again, he'd misjudged her motives so greatly he might assume the payment he'd given her for the diamond would be enough to satisfy her.

Indeed, she'd accepted the money offered to her by Barsegh when he returned her gun, although she didn't intend to keep it for herself. Then she'd taken a circuitous route back to the hotel, doubling back and making many stops, in case he'd followed her.

He'd been as impassive and unreadable as he was from the moment they got to the parlor. Maybe it was a necessity for a man whose employer spoke of him like a dog.

Ellen hid in the shadows of the hedges again and watched the guards. Their patrols deviated ever so slightly from the pattern she'd memorized. A sign of William's caution, no doubt. She'd passed his security once, and so he changed their patrols.

If he expected her to blunder through without taking the time to study their progress again, he was mistaken. It was risky to return to the manor so soon, but it might give her an advantage if he expected her to change her methods. She would not be so foolish as to walk into another trap set by Barsegh, either.

The night dragged on as she watched the guards, until she had a cramp in her calf for crouching so long, but at last she felt secure enough to dart forward and reach the manor wall. As she rubbed the soreness from her leg, a thrill of satisfaction surged through her. Getting the better of a man who thought he could buy her loyalty would be sweet indeed.

Breaking into the gallery would be the trickiest part. It had been nearly unguarded on her first visit, but that was probably a ploy to lure her in. This time he would have heightened security whether or not he anticipated her return.

Ellen crept along the exterior wall of the manor until she found another lightly-guarded entrance and made her way inside.

Indeed, security was much stronger. Guards patrolled the corridors in groups of three, and even the servants who walked through the halls appeared to be on high alert. She waited for an opportunity and then found her way into a tiny room, a storage room from the looks of it.

Once again, patience was key and she resigned herself to a long night of memorizing the interior guards' patrols.

Normally, she allowed herself some degree of risk. It didn't matter if anyone saw her as long as she took them out before they could stop her. She warned her targets ahead of time and left a calling card to tell them she'd won. This time, however, things were different. Her adversary would make good on his threats if he knew she had come for his diamond. It had to be an invisible crime, one that would leave him oblivious.

The interior pocket of Ellen's cape contained not only her tools but also the fake Star Diamond from the trade. She would return the replica to Lord William. It was a gamble, but she had to trust he wouldn't study the diamond too closely in the immediate future. The safe option was to back off and accept her loss, but if Ellen had wanted a safe life, she would be at home sipping tea with friends.

He would eventually discover the deception, of course, but by then Ellen would be far from England where William and Barsegh could not find her and uncover her identity.

Unfortunately, getting into the gallery without being noticed might be impossible. She doubted the guards would ever leave its doors. Any commotion intended to draw them away would be a warning sign that she'd been there.

If only the art gallery had a second door, but there was only one. Disguising herself as a member of the staff was unlikely to work here. The gallery had no windows she could exploit, either, only the skylight…

The skylight. The domed window letting light shine down upon the gallery's centerpiece. Ellen drew a sharp breath. It was the gallery's one vulnerability.

She would need to reach the manor's roof, however, and the exterior walls looked completely smooth. Climbing to the top would be an acrobatic feat beyond her strength and skill. Yet if she could start from a higher point, she might still stand a chance.

With a new plan in mind, the young adventuress used what she had learned of the guards' patrols to leave her hiding place and reach the stairs. Security was lighter there, as no doubt he assumed the gallery would be the focus of any would-be thieves. Ellen crept up to the second floor, and then the third, until at last she prowled in search of an exit that could give her access to the roof.

A window in a maid's empty room opened onto a ledge within reach of the ceiling. Ellen braced herself, then crawled out onto the ledge. After a moment, she lowered the window to make it less conspicuous if anyone entered the room, but she didn't close it entirely to avoid stranding herself outside.

Then she took a breath and hauled her slender frame up to the manor roof.

She must have made quite a sight, a lone figure in a silk gown and fluttering cape framed by the moonlight as she stood upon the clifftop manor. The ocean waves crashed over the rocks so far below, and Ellen found a moment of peace as she caught her breath. Once this was over, she intended to take a legitimate vacation where she could stay firmly on the ground.

From above, finding the gallery was easy. The skylight stood out, a massive dome of glass atop the one room that extended up to the roof. Ellen crept to it and peered down into the gallery.

Six guards protected the art collection, but they all faced away from the exhibits. Their attention was fully focused on the door.

If she could get through the window without drawing their attention, the Star Diamond was as good as hers. Shattering glass would alert them, but she had made silent burglaries in the past.

From her wrist-bag, Ellen withdrew a stick of chewing gum and a small glass cutter. She chewed the gum to make it soft and malleable and then applied it around the edge of one of the glass panes that made up the skylight's faceted design. With the gum in place, she sliced open the window, careful not to damage the glass too much.

Stuck together thanks to the gum, the glass didn't fall. Ellen tilted it toward her with the glass cutter and pried the pane free. Hand wrapped in the cloth of her cape, she grabbed the glass and continued removing the rest with her other hand. At last, it came completely free and opened a path down into the gallery below.

She paused. The guards below didn't move. Satisfied, she produced a coil of rope, secured one end to the roof, and dropped the rest down through the hole she had created.

The climb down was tense, laborious work, with each inch of progress made more alarming by the fact that even a single heavy breath might alert the guards to her presence. Yes, after this was done she would go back to the beach, maybe with Roge this time, and take a nice *long* rest.

Inch by inch, she descended the rope, then dropped silently in front of the Star Diamond's plinth.

After a glance over her shoulder at the oblivious guards, she studied the displayed jewel. Yes, this was the true Star Diamond.

There were no visible traps. Good. She lifted the glass, swapped out the Star Diamond for the replica, secured the jewel within the pocket of her cape, and then returned to the rope to leave Lord William and his gallery behind forever.

From there, the job became almost routine. She slipped past the guards and escaped the manor, then proceeded down the treacherous cliff path to the rocks below. She'd hidden a change of clothes in town far from the hotel where she was staying, so she stopped on the way and removed her telltale white gown and black cape. Dressed instead in a demure green evening gown, Ellen stuffed her costume and mask into her wrist-bag and then continued the rest of the way on foot.

She turned it into an evening stroll and returned to the hotel in high spirits, with a few lighthearted comments for the bellhop on her way inside. Then she froze.

For despite all of her precautions and her firm belief she hadn't been followed, *the man sitting in the lobby was undeniably Barsegh!*

Ellen kept her gait casual as she made her way through the hotel to her room, despite the pounding her heart. Her work as the Domino Lady had given her a particularly keen sixth sense, so she didn't have to turn around to know Barsegh had followed her out of the lobby and remained just behind her.

She half-expected someone to question him, but he shadowed her all the way to her room.

At the door, she turned around and adopted a startled expression, hand over her heart. "Who are you? Why are you following me?"

Barsegh smirked. "You know the answers to both of those questions."

"I'm afraid I don't," she said, looking for all the world like a lady in distress. "Please leave me be, or I will have to call for help."

He shook his head. "Do you really want me to accuse you of being the Domino Lady publicly? Then again, I could just accuse you of theft and find out if you have the Star Diamond with you."

"They'd believe my word over yours," she said.

"But Lord William wouldn't."

She frowned. Barsegh must have followed her either on her previous trip or this one, successfully despite her attempts to throw any pursuers off her trail. Lord William's threats weren't idle, but it seemed Barsegh hadn't yet given her away, even though it would be easy enough for men of their resources to uncover her identity once he learned where she was staying.

"Fine," she said. "We'll talk about this in private."

He smiled again as she unlocked the door to her room and led him inside. "Does this mean you're through dissembling?"

Ellen watched him warily. His motives were still unknown, since he wanted to talk to her privately instead of going straight to his employer. "There would be no point in denying it any longer, would there?"

Even without proof, drawing enough attention to Ellen Patrick as potentially being the Domino Lady would cause a scandal and lead to an investigation. It would destroy her, just as William had threatened. The worst possible scenario had finally come true.

"So you think I've stolen the Star Diamond and you want it back," she said. "Either that or you want to intimidate me into working with Lord William."

"Correction, I *know* you stole the Star Diamond."

She gave him a flat look. "How?"

His grin was almost friendly. "It's what I would have done in your position."

"Does Lord William know?" she asked.

"No."

He left unspoken the obvious conclusion that he would tell his employer if she refused to cooperate.

Ellen sighed and opened her wrist-bag. Everything was hidden in there. The Star Diamond. Her costume. Her tools.

Her gun.

In the gallery, he'd known she wouldn't shoot him. If she drew her gun now, he might think her desperate enough to go through with it. But intimidating him wouldn't accomplish anything. She would have to actually kill him, so that his knowledge would die with him.

If she shot Barsegh, she could claim he had attacked her first. People would believe her.

Yet that would set her on a path she could never return from. Her hands would be stained with blood, and the blood of a man who only threatened to blackmail her, not kill her.

Ellen reluctantly removed the Star Diamond from its hiding place. As repellant as it was to let Lord William win, it was the most palatable of her options. One day she would return and take it back. She would not forget this.

She held it out.

"So that's your answer?" Barsegh asked. "Lord William thought you would kill me."

The possibility didn't seem to bother him at all.

"In fact," he said, "you might fear he predicted, as I did, that you would return for the Star Diamond, but it never occurred to him at all. He assumed you would try to assassinate me for the threat I posed."

"Lord William doesn't have a high opinion of me, does he?" she asked, her voice dry.

"He assumes you think the way he does."

It made Ellen's skin crawl. Whatever they might have in common, she would never work with a man like William Langdale. He hadn't merely considered that she *might* kill Barsegh, but outright *assumed* it would be her first move.

And while she certainly was glad he had let her leave the manor unscathed, he had done so fully believing she would try to murder his associate.

"Why are you loyal to Lord William?" Ellen asked.

Barsegh smiled.

"I know you don't like him," she said. "If I killed you tonight, he'd write it off as the unfortunate loss of a useful tool, and I think you know that. So why?"

"I started working for him because I had no means of my own, and his resources as an employer could put me in a position to get what I wanted."

"Which is what?" she asked.

"What did you intend to do with the Star Diamond?" he asked instead. "You aren't like him. I highly doubt you have a gallery like his."

At this point, there was little reason to lie. "I would hold onto it for a while until the search for it died down," she said, "and then I'd sell it. There are charities near my home where I'd donate the money."

"But it wasn't good enough to accept William's payoff."

"I can't stand to let someone like him get away with what he's done. The Star Diamond can never be returned to its original owner, but I'd rather it not be in his hands either."

Barsegh turned away from her and looked out the window at the night sky. "You asked what it is that I wanted. Let me introduce myself to you formally. My full name is Barsegh Sarafian. My great-grandfather was Jirair Sarafian."

Ellen sat down heavily on the edge of the bed. "You're descended from the original owner of the Star Diamond?"

"Yes."

"Then you aren't going to give it to Lord William?" she asked.

"No. Our partnership is over."

This changed the situation. His voice was sincere, and if he was truly the original owner's great-grandson, he had a greater right to the Star Diamond than anyone else. Ellen held it out once more. "Then it's yours."

Barsegh didn't move. "You would give it to me, after everything you went through to get it?"

"It belongs to you," she said. "Returning it would have been my goal from the start if I knew who you were."

"And since you didn't, you decided to put it toward a good cause."

"Yes."

Barsegh faced her again, but he didn't take the jewel. He studied her, his expression inscrutable. Then he shook his head. "What would I do with a diamond?"

She stared at him.

"I sought the Star Diamond for years. I planned to steal it from the gallery myself, but you were the variable I hadn't planned for. I came here tonight to get the measure of you, and now I understand. You'll do more good work by selling the Star Diamond than I could, and I think my great-grandfather would prefer that to me owning a jewel."

"Are you sure?" she asked. "You are the Star Diamond's rightful owner."

"Then think of it like this," he said. "You have returned it to my family. Thank you. Now I give it to you as a gift. Do with it what you will, and don't worry about William. Before I dissolve our partnership, I'll make sure he believes you still have the fake."

"Thank you," she said.

Barsegh walked to the door and glanced back over his shoulder with a smile. "He sees you as a kindred spirit, but you're something much rarer and more precious than a glory-seeker like him. I hope you continue your work for many years to come."

Then he left, and Ellen sat alone, staring into the depths of the Star Diamond.

"Well," Roge said, as he sat down to eat lunch with Ellen a month later, "the Star Diamond finally resurfaced."

Ellen put her hand over her mouth to feign astonishment. "After all this time?"

"It seems the Domino Lady fenced it and it showed up on the black market. Now Annabelle Lindh is trying to get it back, but things have gotten even more muddled. That Lord William character publicly withdrew his request to buy it and declared the Star Diamond to be a fake. Now folks are saying she never had the Star Diamond and was only pretending to own it for clout."

She laughed. "What a confusing mess."

"You're telling me." Roge shook his head. "All the same, I can't help but be on the Domino Lady's side here. A lot of things are coming out now about just how the Lindh family got that diamond, and… well, I suppose I can't blame the Domino Lady for taking it."

"Are you praising a thief?" Ellen asked.

"Maybe I shouldn't," he said, "but all things considered, I think the Domino Lady had the right of it."

Ellen returned to her lunch with a smile.

After they finished, Roge stood and held out his hand. "Shall we?"

She placed her hand in his and rose from the table. "I'd love to."

Together, they walked to the beach, and Ellen let out a contented sigh. A true vacation was long since overdue.

The End

Domino Lady On Hold

*A*fter writing "The Domino Lady Takes the Case," I knew I wanted to return and write another story about the Domino Lady someday. However, I didn't want to retread the same ground and make my second story another investigation into corruption. This one had to be something different.

Of all the original Domino Lady stories, one that really feels distinct from the others to me is "Emeralds Aboard." It doesn't focus on blackmail or corruption directly, but rather on Ellen's mission to steal a precious set of emeralds.

With that as my inspiration, I decided my new story would also be about stealing a jewel—although of course I didn't want to mimic "Emeralds Aboard" too closely. I settled on the train idea early on, since I wanted Ellen's plan to involve a seemingly impossible heist.

Yet a story solely about Ellen using her wits and resources to steal a jewel would end rather quickly, and it felt too basic. It needed something more to flesh it out into a full story. That was when I decided her efforts would be thwarted by a rival thief.

Why? How would it be resolved? I didn't know, but I wrote the first part of the story, up through Ellen's discovery that the diamond was a fake, and then I stopped.

It was November, and since I always participate in NaNoWriMo, I put my Domino Lady story on hold in order to write the rough draft of a new novel. I didn't like stalling for a whole month in the middle of a draft, but I didn't have enough time to finish it first. So I set it aside and resolved to finish the story when NaNoWriMo ended.

December soon arrived, and I returned to the Domino Lady. I now found myself faced with two problems: it had been a month since I'd even looked at it, and I'd stopped partway through with no plan for the rest. It was time to continue the story, but I had no idea where it was going. The rival thief existed in my thoughts as a shadowy figure named Basile, but what did he want? Why did he steal the diamond? Who was he working for?

Progress stalled yet again as I considered and discarded several ideas, until one day I was watching a movie with Sydney Greenstreet in it and suddenly said to myself, "That's him—that's Basile's employer!" Inspiration is a strange thing, because now that I had a face for my antagonist, Lord William came to life with his motivation and goals.

At this point the entire story was coming together, with William and Basile (whose original name I kept out of convenience for the rest of the draft, even though I had long since stopped picturing him as an Englishman) facing off against the Domino Lady.

The story still needed one last piece to bring everything together, and I wanted it to involve that mysterious rival thief. At last, I made the decision that he was descended from the Star Diamond's original owner. I added that into the plot, finally changed his name (picking Barsegh, which is simply the Armenian variation of the name Basile), and revised his interactions and the history of the diamond accordingly.

Finally, I went through my draft from start to finish and added in some specific styles and phrases that call back to the original Domino Lady stories, which I think helps lend it an air of authenticity.

"The Domino Lady Deceived" traveled a rocky path to completion, but I had fun writing it, and I hope you had fun reading it!

Until we meet again—be it with the Domino Lady or another pulp hero.

SAMANTHA LIENHARD - has been writing for most of her life, especially in the fantasy and horror genres. She graduated from Mansfield University with a B.A. in English and a minor in Creative Writing, and then from Seton Hill University with an M.F.A. in Writing Popular Fiction. When she isn't writing, she can usually be found playing video games. Her publications include a comedy novella called *The Zombie Mishap*, a Lovecraftian horror novella called *The Book at Dernier*, a Lovecraftian horror novelette called *It Came Back*, the pulp fiction story "The Domino Lady Takes the Case," and several short horror stories. She also writes for video games and has worked on the scripts for several indie titles, including *Ascendant Hearts*, *The Trials of Olympus III*, *Two Till Midnight*, and *Eternal Radiance*.--

Information about all of her work can be found at her website: http://www.samanthalienhard.com

DOMINO Lady

Pulpdom's Sexiest Avenger!

The Domino Lady first appeared in the pulps in 1936. After graduating from the Berkeley College in California, Ellen Patrick goes off to Europe on a joy filled jaunt. Her trip is cut short when her widowed father, D.A. Owen Patrick, is murdered by gangsters. Upon her return home she learns the corrupt authorities have no intention of finding her father's killers. Thus she puts on a domino mask and a backless white dress to avenge him. Though arming herself with a small .22 automatic and a syringe full of knockout serum, the Domino Lady's most effective weapon was her sensual beauty, which often distracted her opponents until she could turn the tables on them.

New pulp writers, Greg Hatcher, Gene Moyers, Tim Bruckner and Kevin Findley now offer up four brand new adventures of Los Angeles' most notorious, and sexiest, crime-fighter of them all, the Domino Lady!

Pulpdom's sexiest masked avenger returns in this second volume of her all new adventures. From a gang of corrupt policemen to secret Nazis saboteurs out to destroy the Los Angeles Olympics, the beautiful and wily crime-fighter has her hands full in this new quartet of tales by Gene Moyers, Brad Mengel, Robert Ricci and Paul Findley. As always, lovely socialite Ellen Patrick weaves her way in and out of trouble, donning her black silk domino mask whenever injustice rears its ugly head. From the time of her father's murder, Ellen has dedicated herself to righting wrongs. She just does it in a most peculiar fashion becoming the pulps' most alluring and deadly hero; the Domino Lady.

Pulpdom's sexiest masked avenger returns in five new adventures courtesy of writers Adam Mudman Bezecny, Gene Moyers, Brad Mengel and Samantha Lienhard. By day she is wealthy Los Angeles socialite Ellen Patrick. By night she dons her mask, cape and arms herself with a hypodermic syringe and deadly silver plated automatic to become the beautiful and mysterious vigilante known only as the Domino Lady.

In this volume she uncovers a secret female society also combating evil; a plot to take over rich wineries, confronts a blackmailer, defends a Hollywood union against gangsters and solves a friend's murder. All in a night's work for the one and only, Domino Lady.

PULP FICTION FOR A NEW GENERATION!

Airship27Hangar.com

www.ingramcontent.com/pod-product-compliance
Lightning Source LLC
Chambersburg PA
CBHW051129260626
47170CB00005B/1736